The Return of the Arcane

BY

CELINKA SERRE

EDITED BY CLEO MIELE

COVER BY BINKY INK

BINKY INK

THE LITERARY ARM OF BINKY PRODUCTIONS

WWW.BINKYPRODUCTIONS.COM/THERETURNOFTHEARCANE

<u>Warnings:</u>

Please be advised that this story deals with sensitive topics, such as ageism, which may be offensive to some readers.

Please be advised that one of the characters is an amputee and this may be triggering for some readers.

Other Warnings include:
Strong language, mature subject matter, violence, and blood.

TABLE OF CONTENTS

Arcanus

Arcānus: Arcane.

Arcane: Mysterious, secret, obscure, hidden.

Arcana: Secrets, mysteries; two groups of cards in Tarot, the Major Arcana representing one's spiritual journey.

DRAMATIS PERSONAE

Arthurian Characters:

A.G. (Arthur Gabriel) – *Arthur*
Lance – *Lancelot*
Gen (Geneviève) – *Guinevere*
Aylmer – *Merlin*
Casey – *Kay*
Gad – *Gawain*
Raven – *Aggravain*
Garrick – *Gaheris*
Gareth – *Gareth*
Gallagher – *Galahad*
Devon – *Geraint*
Bedford – *Bedivere*
Boris – *Bors*
Lamar – *Lamorak*
Percy – *Percival*
Tristan – *Tristan*
Isabelle – *Iseult*
Vivian – *Vivian*
Morgan – *Morgan*
Moe – *Mordred*

<u>*Original Characters:*</u>

Okwaho
Sean
Serena

<u>CHAPTER ONE</u>

Almost 1,500 Years Ago, Year 542 A.D.
Kingdom of Camelot

Arthur crawled on all fours, his body battered and bloody. The battlefield around him raged, fire burning the dry terrain, hot smoke filling his nostrils. He lifted his sword to shield himself from the dark sorcery, but his strength gave way. As his grip loosened, Excalibur dropped to the ground and Arthur fell onto his stomach. The pain he felt told him only magic of the light could heal these entropic wounds.

Lancelot ran to Arthur's side, shouting his name as he dropped to his knees. He turned Arthur over to face him, his eyes glistening. Arthur reached up to cup his face.

'My first knight . . .' Arthur dropped his hand, coughing out blood.

Gawain felled an enemy knight before joining them. His hardened visage told Arthur he had not yet forgiven Lancelot. Though Arthur tried to speak, another coughing fit seized him.

'Cousin . . .' he struggled.

The old sorcerer cast a bright spell but was immediately countered by Mordred. Kay's and Lamorak's voices rose over the din as they instructed the other knights to protect their King, to help Merlin, to secure the Queen's safety. Even then, their words seemed jumbled.

Everything around Arthur was quieting, slowing down. The faces of those around him were streaked with tears as his knights fought their enemy, and Arthur knew they now fought for nought.

Something struck Arthur in the chest. He gasped as his vision blurred, and everything darkened.

The dark magic appeared to Arthur as a swirling orb, crackling like lightning – it was choking him. A harsh, whispery voice reverberated inside his mind.

I cannot be destroyed. My purpose is to kill. This is only the beginning of my reign of terror. I shall endure, I shall fester, and when the time is ripe, I, the embodiment of the Arcane, shall return.

Arthur's heart clenched, and he was gone from the world of the living.

* * *

Present Day – Mid-2020s
Canada

A.G. gave himself another once-over in the mirror, unable to tame his ash-blond hair. He sighed, discouraged, and proceeded to ruffle it up in frustration. 'Hmm, not bad.' He chuckled to himself.

Hearing his phone vibrate, he brought it to his ear. 'Casey, what's up?'

'Hey, bro, just calling to make sure you remember lunch.'

A.G. sighed, 'Dude, I forgot *one* time! Anyway, you joining us all at the bar tonight?'

'Yes. *I* don't forget my appointments.'

'Oh my god, Cay.'

Casey laughed, sounding far too pleased for A.G.'s liking. 'Are Gen and Aylmer going to be there too?'

'Yeah, why?'

'Well, I mean, she's your ex who's now dating your friend.'

A.G. shook his head, though was heartened by his adoptive brother's concern. 'We're all on good terms,' he reassured. 'Gen and I broke up over a year ago, and Aylmer asked me if I'd be okay with them dating. They've got my blessing. Besides' – he glanced over at the closed bathroom door where his roommate was taking a shower – 'I've moved on.'

'If it's who I think it is . . .' began Casey.

'Don't even think about it!' A.G. warned.

'Well, now you're putting ideas in my head.'

'Casey?'

His brother chuckled suspiciously. 'The whole gang only gets together once a month. I'm due to have my fun.'

'Yeah, but you see my roommate every time you come over,' hissed A.G. 'So don't go—'

'All right! My meeting's about to start,' Casey interrupted. 'Remember: lunch later. Bye now!' Casey hung up.

'Jerk,' A.G. muttered.

'I hope that wasn't directed at me.'

A.G. looked up as Lance stepped out of the bathroom with nothing but a towel around his waist. A.G. swallowed, feeling a rush of heat.

'It was Casey,' he replied timidly.

'Now I understand.' Lance walked over to his room. He glanced over his shoulder. 'He joining us tonight?'

His roommate's face was so perfectly clean-shaven, it made A.G. self-conscious about his own shave, worried he missed a spot. He hoped he still looked just as handsome as the man before him.

'Yeah.' All A.G. could do was linger in the doorway as he stared at the other man's perfect abs and toned biceps. His wet dark hair falling perfectly by his ears, a trickle of water running down his chest.

Lance paused. 'Everything okay?'

'Lance,' said A.G., 'I, uh . . .' He exhaled, mustering his courage. 'I think I'm in love with you.' He winced internally. *A declaration of love right off the bat?!*

Lance smiled, blushing. 'Yeah?' He bit his lower lip. A.G. held his breath. 'Well, that's good, because as it happens, I feel the same about you.'

A.G. needed a moment to process. Lance chuckled, and before A.G. knew it, the other man's lips were on his. Hands framing each other's faces, A.G. deepened the kiss. Lance's towel fell to the floor and the two men fell onto the bed, their lips never parting.

* * *

'So the probability relative to the components of the fusion makes combustion almost instantaneous!'

Gen stared back at Aylmer, nodding with uncertainty. Aylmer couldn't help but laugh as the two walked hand in hand down the street, fallen leaves crunching beneath their shoes.

'That went way over your head, didn't it?' He pushed up his glasses.

Gen grimaced. 'I'm so sorry. You know I love it when you talk science and physics to me, but I barely understood a single word you said.'

Aylmer stopped and passed a hand through Gen's golden-brown locks. 'What matters to me is just being able to gush about this stuff and bounce ideas off someone else.'

Gen smiled beautifully. Leaning forward, Aylmer gave her a soft kiss. She hummed a sigh and Aylmer pulled away, feeling his cheeks flush. 'Hmmm, *eres asombrosa*.'

'Hmmm, I love it when you speak Spanish.'

Aylmer chuckled. 'Then thank my mother for teaching me her language and culture.' He grinned – he always beamed with pride when sharing his Chilean heritage – and the two resumed. They stopped in front of a large apartment building and sat down on a bench to wait.

And wait . . .

Gen checked her watch. 'Not like them to be late.'

The door at the front of the building slammed open, and A.G. and Lance stumbled out. 'We're here, we're on time!'

'What took you so lo . . .' Aylmer trailed off, clocking how dishevelled both looked – A.G. was still slipping on his jacket, and both were blushing harder than Aylmer had ever seen.

'Ah, finally!' Gen squealed. She jumped up, pulling Lance along. 'Time for work. See you two tonight!'

Lance made doe eyes at A.G. as Gen started firing off questions, the two of them already walking away.

Aylmer sighed, 'And in her excitement, she forgot to kiss me goodbye.' He let out a laugh, pulling A.G. along as they began in the opposite direction. He nudged him with his elbow. 'You look happy.'

A.G. smiled shyly. 'Yeah, I am . . . told him this morning how I felt.'

Aylmer nodded. 'Well, seeing as yesterday you were still pining hopelessly, probability is you told him sometime between last night and this morning, and judging how the two of you were acting just now, I observe that he reciprocated.'

'Very much so,' breathed A.G.

Aylmer hissed a laugh. '*Es suficiente.* Please, I don't need the details.'

Laughing, A.G. nodded as the two headed to work.

* * *

Crossing the floor, Gad snapped his fingers. 'Gareth, get us an appointment with the investors.'

Gareth rolled his eyes. 'Oh my god, Gad, you're so pushy today.'

'Owning a business means we're allowed to slack off sometimes.' Garrick rolled up his sleeves and folded his arms, giving Gad a pointed look.

'First of all, it's "Oh my *Gad*," Gareth,' Gad began.

'Not this again . . .' Gareth muttered, pinching the bridge of his nose.

'Now, as an *owner* of this business,' Gad continued.

Raven watched, looking amused, while Gareth somehow rolled his eyes even further back.

Garrick laughed, his low voice echoing off the shop walls. 'You do remember we all have equal shares in this business, yes?' He placed his sawing board beside the table he'd been working on and tested his newly finished chair. He reclined, folding his arms and giving Gad one of those looks Gad knew *he* knew he hated.

'As the eldest, then,' Gad insisted.

Raven stepped forward, gesturing to himself and the elaborate tattoos covering his arms. 'Yet it was *me* who won the Sexiest African-Canadian Business Owner of the Year Award, contributing to our enterprise's popularity.' He grinned, his white teeth sparkling. He brought his hand to his mouth and mimicked the sound of sparkles.

Gad sighed, tracing his goatee with his index finger and thumb. Discouraged by his brothers' teasing, he threw his arms up in surrender. 'I give up.'

'There we go!' Garrick whooped with enthusiasm, standing. He walked over to Gad and started rubbing the elder brother's shoulders. 'Gotta learn to relax, Gad. These furnishings won't run away before we're done.'

'Yeah, yeah, all right,' Gad conceded, tension leaving his shoulders at once. 'It *is* Friday, after all, and we *are* meeting with the others tonight. Might as well leave it till Monday.'

Garrick and Raven cheered with a loud 'Yay!'

'Do keep on massaging, though, oh fabulous brother of mine.'

After a few more motions, rubbing into the knot in Gad's back, Garrick stopped.

'Gad,' Gareth hesitated, a serious look on his face. 'Please don't snap your fingers at me. *She* . . . used to do that.'

'Oh shit, I'm so sorry!' Gad immediately closed the distance and wrapped his arms protectively around his youngest brother, feeling stupid for not realising.

'It's okay, I'm over it. But sometimes . . . things she said or did to me . . . just . . .'

'I get it,' Gad reassured him, pulling back. A silent understanding passed between them. Gad loved his brothers. He'd do anything to protect them all, including helping them heal from abusive exes.

'How about we close up shop,' suggested Raven, 'and make a reservation for tonight?'

'Right, Lance did ask me if I could take care of that.' Gad rubbed his hands together. 'Table for sixteen, it shall be.'

'Let's hope they give us one of the round booths. They're the comfiest,' said Garrick.

Together, the four brothers headed out.

* * *

The way Casey was staring at A.G. from across their small table was making him uncomfortable. His head was inclined forward, making his thick eyebrows look more pronounced with the way his dark hair fell towards them, and in his eyes was expectation. A.G.

just knew his adoptive older brother wanted *all* the details.

'I thought you'd be satisfied with that.'

'No way! I want to know his reaction.'

'I told you!' A.G. insisted. 'He smiled, said he felt the same, and kissed me.'

'Did he blush? Did you hesitate?' With each new question, Casey leaned further forward, his eyes widening. 'What was he wearing?'

'A bath towel,' A.G. replied pointedly. Casey paused, mouth open over his sandwich. 'Until it fell. And then—'

'Okay, got it! No need to go into TMI territory.'

A.G. waved his hand, exasperated, but he couldn't suppress the chuckle that followed.

Casey made a face as he chewed, and A.G. followed his line of sight to the tall woman in heels and a tight expensive-looking outfit strutting their way. Her dark hair was perfectly coiffed and her makeup accentuated her sharp features.

'Fancy seeing you here . . . *not.*'

'Hi, Morgan.' A.G. tried to smile, but it came out as strained as hers.

'A.G.' She looked at Casey. 'Casey.' The older woman flung her long wavy black hair over her shoulder. 'I see the two of you still have no qualms living as' – she contorted her face in disdain – 'middle-class rabble. Makes me embarrassed just knowing you're my half-brother, A.G.'

'Good for you, Morgan,' A.G. replied sarcastically. The older woman scrutinised him a bit longer before plastering another fake smile on her face. 'I'll see you around.' And with that, she strutted off.

Casey pointed a thumb her way. 'She knows you know she hates you, right?'

A.G. sighed. 'It's complicated. Sometimes we get along, though something tells me it's more for our father's benefit than mine.'

'Do you sometimes wish you hadn't searched for your biological family?'

A.G. sighed again. 'I don't know. Morgan isn't *so* bad. It's her son who can do no wrong in her eyes who's the real problem.'

'Tell me about it!' groaned Casey. 'How old is he now, eighteen? And how many times has he been arrested for getting into altercations?'

'Don't get me started.'

'Then tell me more about this morning – skipping the TMI portion.'

A.G. chuckled and shook his head. Yet even now, he was missing Lance.

* * *

Lance found his mind drifting to A.G. and felt heat rise to his face. He just could not focus on the code he was supposed to be writing.

'What's got you grinning like a madman?' Gallagher asked, leaning forward and practically off his desk.

Lance shook the replay of that morning's love declarations from his mind.

'Lance and A.G. finally got together,' Gen piped up.

'Oooh, look at you, stud!' Percy whooped.

'And I hear what followed was *mind-blowing*,' Gen went on.

Lance felt so hot, he just knew his face was beet red.

'Pop's got a boyyfrieeend!' Gallagher sing-songed, bobbing his head from side to side, his neat brown hair swaying in the air.

'Was about time,' Percy muttered.

Lance couldn't help but grin. 'Thanks, guys. It means a lot to have your support.'

'Of course!' said Percy. 'You and A.G. go *way* back. You're the OGs of the gang. We all saw it, how much you two care for each other.'

'He's been my best friend for so long,' said Lance. 'He was the first person I came out to as bi – we bonded over it. I think I always had a thing for him before I even knew it.'

'Is *that* why you were so jealous when he and I started dating?' asked Gen, grinning.

'God, yes!' admitted Lance. 'I mean, we'd both been crushing on you, but then *he* got you, and that's when I realised I had feelings for *him.*'

'It's a good thing we broke up, then,' teased Gen. 'Love you both, but it just wasn't working out. You know what they say about "meant to be!"' She winked.

'Why did you wait so long, though?' asked Gallagher.

Lance shrugged. 'I think it was fear. There was always a reason to put it off.' His eyes unfocused as he reminisced. 'I wanted to tell him so badly.' Smiling, he bit his lip. 'It was him who said it this morning.'

'Good!' Gallagher grinned. 'Pop was taking too long.'

'Are you ever going to stop calling me Pop?' asked Lance, feeling too much longing for A.G. that only grew the more they talked about him. 'I'm just, what, a dozen years older than you . . . you graduate rook,' he teased back.

'Well, you did take me in off the street – literally. Lance . . .' Gallagher grew serious. 'I had no one, and nowhere to go – I was sleeping on park benches because I was kicked out of foster care at eighteen. I was alone, and then you came along. You helped me, let me live with you, taught me how to code, and now I've got my life back on track. I'll always be grateful to you for that. You're the closest thing to family I've got, that I've ever had.' He beamed at Lance. 'So no, I'll never stop calling you Pop.'

It warmed Lance's heart that the young twenty-year-old man regarded him as such. He smiled.

'It did help that his good friend – that's me, by the way,' – Percy pointed at himself – 'is the manager and got the top boss to agree to the new hire. Which reminds me: get back to work, you three!'

Gen clicked her tongue as Percy chuckled to himself. Lance tried to refocus on the code.

'Hey Lance,' Gallagher whispered. As Lance looked over, the young man gave him a thumbs-up. 'I'm really happy for you and A.G.'

'Tcht!' Percy lifted his ginger head above his screen.

Lance hid behind his own monitor, but focusing was one dragon he would not slay today.

* * *

Moving a long strand of blond hair away from his face, Lamar shut the door to his apartment and looked over at Tristan, who did the same.

'Isabelle not joining us?' asked Lamar.

'Not tonight,' replied Tristan. His tawny face was aglow with joy.

'Look at you,' said Devon, approaching from down the hall. His sharp, upturned dark eyes held a hint of blue, face framed by straight black hair that fell neatly along his ears – features reflecting his Korean descent from his father's side. 'So in love! Engagement suits you.'

'Thanks, Doc, but being a married man will suit me better.'

'Ah,' said Boris as he descended the stairs. 'Glad you could join us, Devon.'

'Me too. My shift ended with no emergencies. All patients were well taken care of.' Devon looked at his wristwatch. 'And I'm off duty for the next few days, so I can drink tonight.'

'Fantastic!' said Lamar. 'We're just missing Bedford.' He pointed at his apartment behind him. 'He was finishing up a call.'

Devon folded his arms. 'Well, I can say I sure am glad you chose to stay, Tristan, and not elope like you wanted to do.'

Tristan chuckled. 'Isa and I are both glad we stayed, too.'

'And you're not getting too much trouble from, uh . . . ?' Lamar asked, lifting his brows. Tristan shook his head.

The door behind Lamar opened and out walked Bedford, looking suave. He had put gel in his textured cropped hair, which somehow made his facial hair seem neater. His shirt collar was pulled up, sticking out of his jacket.

'You look smart,' said Boris.

'I'm feeling lucky tonight.' Bedford chuckled. 'Maybe I'll meet a beautiful lady.'

He wasn't wearing his prosthetic, Lamar noted. Bedford had lost his hand in an accident several years back. He had prosthetics for ease at home, but he was comfortable going out without them most of the time.

'Tristan,' Lamar began as the group headed out, returning to their previous conversation, 'you're a damn lucky fool. To be with Isabelle, the way you two got together . . .'

'Yeah, man,' said Bedford, 'who does that? Go pick up your boss's fiancée at the airport, start an affair with her, plan to elope, and then, what, he found out and *didn't* fire you?'

'Only because he was having an affair, too!' rebutted Tristan. 'It was love at first sight. What can I say? I *am* lucky, though – things could've become real nasty fast otherwise.'

'Love sounds so complicated,' said Boris. 'I'm good over here in my asexual corner. The only thing to worry about is which of my pals will foot the bill.' The group laughed.

'Or are we going to run into those bikers?' muttered Bedford.

'You know I can defeat them anytime,' Lamar boasted, recalling the time he single-handedly fought off ten of them. He flexed, feeling powerful. Tristan playfully shoved him.

As they entered the bar, they saw Gad and the brothers, and learned entrées had already been ordered. Lamar's stomach gurgled. 'Thank goodness for nachos.'

* * *

Gad stood from his seat as A.G., Aylmer, Lance, Gen, Casey, Percy, and Gallagher all strode in.

'Ah, my best friend arrives at last!' Gad clasped hands with Lance. 'You're awfully smiley today.'

Lance blushed. 'Yeah, well . . .' He looked over at A.G., and from his gaze alone Gad deduced. 'A.G. and I . . .' He lowered his gaze timidly.

'Finally!' Gad cheered. 'Gentlemen and lady, tonight we celebrate' – he elongated his words – '*looong-awaited looove.*' The group whooped and roared, stomping the floor and banging the round booth's table. A.G. blushed more intensely than Lance.

'You'd think they were the ones getting married and not me,' Tristan teased.

Percy and Lamar chuckled as these two brothers conferred with each other.

Amid the joyful chaos, one of the waitresses – a middle-aged woman with a Southern accent – walked over to their booth. 'Howdy, boys.' She winked and flashed her signature smile – it always made Gad's stomach do somersaults. 'How are my favourite customers?'

'All the better to have seen you, Vivian,' Raven flirted. Gad sent him a pointed glare. *He* was the one who always flirted with her.

'Oh my!' The woman blushed, patting her well-tied bun. 'You sure do make an old lady feel young again.'

'Come on, you're not old,' Percy chimed in.

'Much older than you know.'

'Then what's your secret?' asked Garrick with a sly smile.

'Swimming, I reckon.' Vivian shrugged. 'Now, tell me, are my chugging champions going to be participating in the next contest?' She narrowed her eyes. 'Our best competitor, the resto-bar half a mile downstreet, also has champions, and we're damn sure not gonna let them take the lead we've had for so long.'

'Sorry,' said Percy, 'but the hangover that followed lasted me a full week. I am not doing it again.'

'Well, our hope lies with our champions, and all three of them are sittin' at this booth.' Vivian waited expectantly.

'You know,' began Gallagher, 'every time I drink at home, I drink from my trophy.'

'Ew, you *drink* from that thing?' Gen asked with disdain.

'What?' Gallagher defended. 'It's a golden goblet made to look like a beer goblet. It's *made* for beer!'

'Yeah, I'm not entirely sure how hygienic that is,' said Aylmer. 'The amount of bacteria . . . ugh.' He shuddered at the thought.

'Well, I don't drink from mine,' stated Boris, 'nor do I intend to participate again. Nearly wiped me out last time.'

'Gallagher'll do it!' Lance cheered him on. 'You're the youngest of us here. Your stomach's made of steel.'

'Sure, Pop, I'll do it.'

Everyone cheered.

'I'll bring over the inscription form, then,' said Vivian, smiling. She took their orders and left the booth.

The gang began to properly settle in, updating each other on all the latest from the past weeks and enjoying each other's company as they always did – until the loud rev of motorcycles outside quieted them.

Gad sighed, bringing his hand to his forehead. 'I swear, if Moe and his gang come in here . . .'

As if summoned, the bar-n-grill's doors slammed open with a loud bang. Obnoxious yelling followed as the young men sauntered over to a nearby booth as if they owned the place. Vivian was already issuing warnings.

Moe meandered to their booth, leaning an elbow on the backrest. 'Sup, losers! You old men really should stop acting like you're half your age. You're embarrassing today's youth.'

'I suppose that makes me old, too?' Gallagher concluded.

'You deserve better than to hang out with a bunch of old men,' scoffed Moe. 'My offer still stands, if you want to save your skin and jump ship.'

'No thanks.'

'I'd dispense with the ageism, brat!' Percy warned.

'And you!' Moe pointed at Gen, ignoring Percy. 'It really doesn't help your complexion to hang around such men. You look like an old hag – your beauty's fading.'

Percy stood abruptly, stepping menacingly towards Moe. 'You dare insult the lady?'

Moe guffawed. 'Lady? More like *tramp*.'

Percy pulled his fist back. A.G. stood from the edge of the booth before anyone could strike anyone and stepped between them, putting his arms out.

'Oh, yeah?' Moe taunted. 'You want to take me on, old man? You want to take on an eighteen-year-old?'

Lamar cracked his knuckles, following A.G. and taking a step forward. 'You really want a repeat of last time?'

'That's enough!' shouted A.G. 'Moe, I'd advise you to behave. We don't want any trouble.'

'Or what? You gonna tell my mother?' He feigned worry. 'Ooh, I'm shaking in my boots!'

'Settle down, Moe, now!' A.G. commanded. 'That's an order.'

Moe burst into laughter, turning to his group. 'D'you see his face when he said that? He actually takes himself seriously.'

Vivian marched over to Moe, her usual warm demeanour replaced by an icy glower. 'The police are on their way, and I'm told you're on probation.' She narrowed her blue eyes and, pointing towards the exit, thundered, 'Unless you want to be put back behind bars, boy, you'll leave.'

Moe brought his arms up in surrender. 'It's all just a misunderstanding, officer,' he said, putting on an innocent tone. 'All these old men ganging up on poor little ol' me! My uncle was urging them on. I had to defend myself.' He laughed hideously.

'What the fuck is wrong with you?' breathed Gad.

'Come on, guys, let's go. I feel myself ageing just standing here.' Moe and his gang walked out of the bar, but not before pilfering a handful of fries from one of their plates and grabbing some toothpicks from the hostess stand. The door banged against the wall again, then the motorbikes revved.

As the sound of the engines faded into the distance, everyone slowly sat back down.

'I don't know what his problem is,' sighed A.G.

Gad looked up at Vivian, who had already read his mind. 'I put your orders in to go,' she said. 'Don't worry about the bill.'

'You're a gem, Viv,' said Gad. She smiled, though this time it was strained.

* * *

After leaving the bar-n-grill, they took their meals to Casey's – his place had the most space.

Aylmer was still feeling unnerved and abnormally hot when they stepped towards the dining table. His hand kept tingling. He looked down at it. 'Does my hand look redder than usual to you guys?'

Gen took his hands in hers. He averted her gaze. 'Aylmer? Why won't you look at me?'

'Because I'm pathetic,' he spat. 'Some eighteen-year-old insults my girlfriend and I can't even defend her.'

'Is that what's bothering you?' Gen tenderly tucked a few strands of Aylmer's light-brown hair behind his ear.

That, and the weird discomfort he was experiencing in his body.

'To be fair,' began Percy, 'I was quick on the defending switch.'

'But that shouldn't have stopped me,' argued Aylmer. 'I should be able to defend my girlfriend to some jerk who—'

'Ah!' Gen abruptly retracted her hands, her eyes wide.

Aylmer glanced down. His hand felt like it was on fire. Suddenly, he realised his entire body was trembling.

'Step away,' he warned. 'I don't know what's happening to me!'

It was as though a part of him knew without understanding it. He closed his hand into a fist, somehow knowing it would stop the burning . . . the fire.

Afraid, he gaped at his friends, aware that they were all speaking, aware their tone was that of concern. And then . . .

Aylmer curled in on himself, crying out, as something inside him pulsed, and a shockwave sent everyone sprawling to the floor.

Chapter Two

Aylmer's eyes were wide with fear as his body shook. Gen rose to her feet, reflexively running towards him.

'Don't!' he cried, tears speckling his eyes. 'I . . . I don't know what's happening. I'm so sorry!'

'We're okay, mate,' voiced Garrick.

Slowly, Gen reached for Aylmer. He opened the palm of his hand and a large flame came to life.

'Spontaneous combustion!' cried Gallagher. He grabbed a jug of water from the fridge and doused Aylmer, drenching him, but the flame was not affected.

A.G. cursed under his breath.

'This goes beyond any physics I know,' said Aylmer, bringing the flame closer to his face – it didn't even fog up his glasses. 'Science can't explain it!' He closed his hand with a flourish, and the flame disappeared. 'That's not all. I sort of know how to control it, but I don't know *how* I know.'

He opened his palm again, and this time a blue flame danced in it before he waved both hands about, creating a luminescent barrier that quickly faded from existence.

Gen smiled and placed her hand on Aylmer's face. 'I'm not afraid.' She kissed him gently, and as she felt his body relax, he collapsed to the floor, panting. Gen yelped.

'I'm okay, just feeling a little weak.'

'So . . .' began Casey, 'I have the strangest feeling – kind of like a memory – that A.G. and Gen were once engaged.'

'But we never were,' began Gen, yet even as she said it, she felt Casey's words were true. 'We weren't even dating for that long.'

'I don't know why, but I feel as though when I went to get Isa from the airport,' said Tristan, 'I was . . . on a boat.'

'I feel angry,' expressed Gad. 'At Lance.'

'What did *I* do to you?'

'You . . . you . . . I'm not sure, but I am . . .' His face contorted. 'It's like a distant memory, but it feels so real.'

'Explain how I can do this.' Aylmer waved his hands again, and colourful swirls danced above his head. 'I don't even know what these things are or what they do, but I can do them. How the fuck am I doing this? *What the fuck am I doing?!*'

'Aylmer,' said A.G., 'you need to pulse again. When you did just now, something happened to us. It . . . it feels as though we need this.' The others nodded in agreement.

'Are you mad?!' cried Aylmer. '*¡Dios mío!* I could kill you all, as far as I know!'

'Aylmer,' Gen said softly, 'I believe in you. I trust you.'

'*¡Mi dulce amor, no!* Geneviève, I don't trust *myself!*'

'But what if that pulse thing you did helps us make sense of what's going on right now?' insisted Gen. Something inside her knew that this was what they needed, that it was safe.

'As far as I know,' said Bedford, touching his temple with two fingers, 'we're here tripping balls real intensely – and I've done LSD. This . . . this is something else. I've got two distinct memories of how I lost my hand. One is so vivid, yet so impossible.'

'Aylmer, I know you're scared,' began Gen.

'I'm freaking the fuck *out!*' shouted Aylmer.

'But you need to pulse for us,' Gen went on.

'That's what she said!'

Everyone stared at Percy, stunned silent for a moment, and then they all burst out laughing.

'This is crazy!' laughed Percy.

'What a trip!' Raven shook his head.

'You think Viv slipped something into our drinks?' asked Gallagher.

'Pretty sure that'd land her in jail,' chuckled Casey.

'Aggravating, insane . . .' Gad stared at Raven.

'What?'

'Aggra . . . v . . .' Gad put a hand to his head, swaying.

Gen gently took Aylmer's hand. 'Something is happening – something is changing.' She could feel it, though she could not explain it. 'We need answers, and you hold the key.'

A.G. took Aylmer's other hand. 'We're here to support you in this.'

'You make it sound like I'm a freak,' complained Aylmer.

'Sorry.' A.G. grimaced sheepishly. 'It's as though I know it'll help us. Whatever's happening, it's happening to *all* of us. So let's discover what this is . . . together!'

'Arthur, that's insane!' cried Aylmer.

A.G. blinked. 'No one ever calls me Arthur.'

'Except for Dad,' said Casey. 'When he scolds you or has important matters to discuss.'

'Yeah, but he calls me Arthur Gabriel.'

Aylmer was breathing heavily. Gen reached her other hand out towards Boris, who nodded and reached out to Bedford, who offered him his stump. A.G. caught on and took Lance's hand, who took Casey's, taking Gad's. Each of them linked together, standing in a circle.

Gen rubbed her thumb over Aylmer's knuckles, just as he had for her many times, hoping it would convey reassurance. He met her eyes, looking like a lost puppy.

'I love you,' she whispered.

As Aylmer's face hardened with resolve, she felt something emanate from him, more than she knew to describe. It was at once exhilarating as it was inspiring. Gen nodded back.

Aylmer closed his eyes, breathing in deeply and standing tall. Everyone repeated words of encouragement.

'We're all here.'

'We're in this together.'

'We trust you.'

'If you all die because of me . . .' Aylmer muttered under his breath. Resolved, he puffed out his chest, and a shockwave shook the room.

* * *

Hands gripping tighter, A.G. held on to Lance as flashes passed through his mind of a life from centuries past. He staggered, bringing Lance with him, but regained his footing quickly. It was overwhelming – emotions were running high – and then all at once he felt calm, and he knew. He knew who he was, though not why he had returned.

He opened his eyes, and he could tell from everyone's expressions, they, too, knew.

Aylmer seemed collected and in control, almost meditative.

A.G. turned to Lance immediately, taking his roommate's hands and bringing them to his heart. 'Lance.'

Lance stared at him, looking as nervous as he felt.

He kissed the man's fingers, certain Lance could feel, if not hear, his drumming heart. 'I want you to know that whoever we were in our past lives, it doesn't change how I feel about you now or how I've felt about you for so long.'

'It's the same for me,' replied Lance. A.G. exhaled in relief. 'I love you. I should have told you sooner. Our lives now . . .'

A.G. found himself smiling in earnest, and when Lance leaned forward with a sweet kiss, reassurance washed over him. As they pulled away, A.G. became aware of Gad seething at Lance, hands balled into fists.

'Gad?' Lance attempted.

'You got them killed,' Gad growled.

Lance opened his mouth to speak, then shut it again, sorrow reflected in his eyes.

'We're alive again now, though, so it's all good,' offered Gareth. 'We've been given a second chance. Somehow, through magic.'

'And,' added Garrick, 'it wasn't his fault.' He walked over to his older brother and put a hand on his shoulder. 'That was then, in our past lives, and this is now. And in our current lives, we're alive.'

Lance took a step towards Gad. 'I asked then, but I'll ask again in this life, too.' He brought a fist to his heart before he knelt on one knee, bowing his head. 'Please, forgive me for the error that led to the deaths of your brothers.'

Gad put a hand to his mouth, blinking back tears. 'I need . . . I need more time.'

Lance nodded and rose. The group, still standing in a circle, grew quiet.

'Fucking A!' exclaimed Bedford as Aylmer finally opened his eyes. 'Aylmer! You're fucking *Merlin!*'

Aylmer fired off a series of expletives in Spanish.

As realisation dawned on each of them, they began to question what this meant.

'Does Morgan know?'

'Does Moe?'

'Is it only *us* who are affected?'

'Why now?'

'Why *us?*'

The weight of it all, the burden of past responsibilities, suddenly weighed heavily on A.G.'s shoulders, and he found it hard to breathe.

'I need some air.'

Without looking behind him, he bolted from the house and out into the frigid night.

* * *

'A.G., wait!' Lance called out, rushing after his boyfriend. He grabbed A.G.'s arm as he caught up to him and turned him around, worry written on his face. He searched A.G.'s eyes.

'It's just so overwhelming, Lance.'

'I know.'

'I died! I was *killed*. And now I'm back – why?'

'I don't have the answer to that,' admitted Lance. 'I watched you die. I – I held you, and those memories, with the feelings I have for you in this life . . .' Lance's eyes stung. He turned his gaze away.

'I understand.' A.G. started off again and called over his shoulder, 'Go back upstairs. I just need to clear my head.'

'I'm not leaving your side,' insisted Lance, jogging to reach his side again.

'I'll be fine!'

'My job is to protect you!' Lance emphasised.

A.G. whirled on him. 'Your job is to be my boyfriend!'

The two men stood silent.

Lance leaned in until their foreheads met, tears finally flowing. 'I already lost you once, Arthur, and those flashes broke my heart.' He placed his hands on A.G.'s face as the mere mention of their past life memories knotted his stomach with pang after pang. 'I love you. I'm not losing you again.'

'You won't,' A.G. reassured, 'because I no longer am Arthur. Perhaps I was then, but I'm A.G. Arthur Pendragon is long dead.' He swallowed. 'Fine, so we're reincarnations – so what? You're a programmer and the man I love. I'm a retail store manager. That's it.'

He lowered his voice. 'I'm not a King. You're not my First Knight. We're just two ordinary men, lovers and roommates, and that's what we're going to continue to be.'

A.G. turned to leave, but Lance stopped him. 'So you're just going to ignore everything we experienced tonight?'

'Right on!' A.G. broke Lance's hold and resumed at an even faster pace.

'You can't! We can't ignore what happened. What if there's a deeper meaning to this? You can't just pretend—'

'I am the King! I can do precisely what I want!' A.G.'s eyes widened as he realised what he'd just blurted. He shook his head and kept on, never slowing his stride.

'A.G., please,' Lance implored as he followed.

They turned the corner and bumped into someone. He was tall, with black hair tied into a ponytail and a feather hanging from the tie-up. The stranger clutched his upper arm, gritting his teeth as he hurried past them. Lance scowled.

A.G. looked down at the hand he'd raised before colliding with the man, rubbing his thumb and fingers together, and Lance saw it. 'Blood,' A.G. whispered.

The two instinctively turned back, pursuing the stranger. They found the man leaning against the wall a few paces away, breathing raggedly and groaning in pain. His hand was bloody, and it appeared the laceration went right across his bicep.

A.G. looked the man in the eyes. 'We're gonna get you help, okay?' He pulled out his phone. 'Devon, downstairs, now! Slash across the arm, heavy bleeding. . . . No, not us, we're fine.'

Lance knew the drill, having seen Devon work before. 'Name, age?'

'Name's Okwaho,' the man replied. He winced and let out a moan. 'Twenty-seven . . . I'm fine. If I can just . . .' He groaned loudly as he pushed away from the wall and curled in on himself. Something in the way he tried to dismiss them made Lance suspicious.

'You're clearly not fine!' insisted A.G. as blood trailed down the man's jacket and dripped onto the sidewalk.

The door burst open, and Devon was barking orders to Aylmer. 'I got it!' the sorcerer replied.

Devon pressed some gauze over the wound and instructed the man to remove his jacket. 'I'm a doctor. I'm going to get you patched up.' Once the sleeve was free, Devon began bandaging the wound, wrapping gauze around the man's arm. 'This will help stop the bleeding. I need to take you to the hospital – looks like you're going to need stitches.'

Okwaho nodded.

Devon led them to his car and tossed the keys to Lance. 'You're driving.'

'Got it.'

* * *

After the five of them entered the car, Aylmer tried to pinpoint what exactly it was he was sensing about the man as Lance pressed on the gas.

'How did this happen?' asked Devon, putting pressure on the already blood-drenched bandage. He turned his head to Aylmer. 'I need more gauze.'

'I was attacked,' said Okwaho through gritted teeth.

'By whom?'

'Some punk . . . biker teen.'

'Moe?' cried A.G.

'That's the name.'

Devon finished wrapping more gauze around the wound, applying more pressure as he held the man's arm up above heart level. 'We're almost there.'

Aylmer and A.G. shared a glance. Aylmer's stomach twisted into a knot. 'Why would Moe be after you?'

'I don't know.'

Aylmer waved his hand about, a large diamond-shaped crystalline light glowing from it as he turned his palm towards the stranger. 'He's lying.'

Okwaho's head snapped towards Aylmer. 'You're a sorcerer.'

'Sí. And from what my magic tells me, so are you.'

Yet this man wasn't someone any of them had previously known.

A.G. narrowed his eyes. 'Start talking, *now*.'

CHAPTER THREE

Okwaho flinched, hissing in pain.

'Up this way?' Lance asked as he turned the car onto an accessway.

'Yes, follow that lane to the emergency,' Devon replied, still applying pressure to the gash.

'Are you certain?' A.G. asked Aylmer.

'Without a doubt. This man's a sorcerer.'

'All right, pal, time to start talking.' A.G. fixed Okwaho with a stare. 'Who are you? Why would Moe be after you?'

Devon turned to A.G. once the car stopped. 'Stitches first, talking after.'

A.G. opened his mouth to argue, but Aylmer placed a hand on his shoulder in caution. As Devon helped Okwaho out of the car and ushered him towards the hospital's emergency entrance, Aylmer whispered in A.G.'s ear, 'Trust your knights. You once had a whole council of them. Also, doctor's orders.'

A.G. relented. 'I don't even know why we've been reincarnated or what purpose remembering will bring.'

'It's a lot to process. For all of us,' Aylmer admitted.

They heard Devon telling someone, 'Laceration across the arm. He's going to need stitches. I can treat him.'

'Your call, Doctor Seong.'

Aylmer turned to A.G. 'I'll go with him. Make sure our new friend doesn't try anything.' He hurried out of the car and after Devon and Okwaho, leaving A.G. and Lance to park the car.

When Aylmer glanced behind him, however, A.G. and Lance were standing outside of the vehicle, with Lance holding an agitated A.G. by the shoulders and A.G. leaning away as though he wanted to follow.

* * *

In the emergency room, Aylmer remained quiet while Devon and a nurse cleaned the gash. Okwaho whinged loudly with each touch.

Devon looked over the man's chart. 'Aylmer, can you step out for a moment? I have a few questions I need to ask my patient.'

Aylmer understood that confidentiality with their new acquaintance's medical history needed to be respected. He stepped out for the few minutes required of him, and when he returned, Okwaho asked the nurse for water. As soon as she stepped out of the room, Okwaho began talking at a hundred kilometers per hour.

'The knife that kid used was poisoned.'

'Poisoned?!' exclaimed Devon. He spun around, reaching for a bottle Aylmer assumed was intended for such situations.

'Nothing lethal. It's not anything you can cleanse. But it has . . . rendered my powers useless. Temporarily.' Okwaho opened the palm of his hand, where a faint spark of purple died as quickly as it had appeared. 'He was sent to subdue my magic. I don't think he even knows what his master was asking of him.'

'His master?'

'For people who seem to already know this Moe kid, and especially for a sorcerer, you know very little about those who might threaten you.'

As the nurse returned, Aylmer only had more questions than before, but before long the Mohawk man was stitched up, bandaged, and discharged. Equally confused, Devon suggested they return to Casey's and have their chat with Okwaho there.

* * *

Gad paced to and fro as the group waited as instructed for Aylmer, A.G., Devon, and Lance to return with their new friend. He passed a hand over his face.

'There's no point in hating Lance for *two* lifetimes,' said Garrick.

Gad whirled on his brother. 'He's the reason you and Gareth died!'

'It was a tactical miscalculation,' argued Gareth. 'He didn't know we were among the fighters.'

'I'm certain had he known, he would have issued a different order,' said Raven.

'But we lost two of our brothers!'

'A lifetime ago! A whole millennia and a half ago. We've reincarnated,' insisted Raven.

'Whatever the reason for our return,' began Garrick, 'we've been given a second chance. All of us.'

'I agree,' said Lamar. 'There's no point being bitter about the mistakes of our past lives. Somehow, we're all back – the Knights of the Round Table, returned and reunited. We need to protect our King.'

A surge of anger passed through Gad. 'Are you blaming *me* for his death?'

'I think Lamar was merely stating a fact,' offered Boris. 'But let's not forget history or how the legend claims Mordred found his opening due to rifts between us. Now we have the chance to mend those rifts before it's too late.'

'That's assuming Moe and Morgan don't know who they really are,' said Casey, 'and if they do, then they already have an advantage for having vanquished us once before.'

Gareth, Garrick, and Raven offered Gad a group hug. Just then, the door opened and the others filed in. Lance stopped in front of Gad.

Gad looked at his brothers. They were right, of course – they were alive again, in new bodies, in a different country, in a different time – but the memory had opened that old wound again. It felt fresh and raw, and Gad was not ready to let go. Not tonight.

Lance must have sensed that, for the man cast his eyes to the floor and stepped away. Gad felt a pang in his heart. Lance was his best friend, and he'd been so in their former lives as well. He wanted to forgive him – truly, he did – but the sorrow was too great.

* * *

Okwaho stared at the overwhelming group before him as the tall blond man – A.G. – made the introductions. Despite Okwaho's magic being temporarily subdued, he could sense the verity of their words and knew he could trust them, all of them. In fact, he felt that he *must* trust them, and that they needed him as much as he needed them – magic told him that much, as though some crucial moment had arisen.

A.G. presented each of his friends before ending with, 'Moe is my nephew – half-nephew.'

Okwaho let out a low whistle.

The man he believed was named Casey led everyone back to his living room, where many couches and chairs awaited them. Many of the others scrutinised Okwaho as they went. He glanced down at his stitched arm where the bandage covered a large portion of his wolf tattoo. The localised anesthetic had numbed the pain . . . somewhat. Okwaho sat down on a chair near the entrance, uncertain of where to begin.

'Can we trust him?' asked one of the umber men while the others, spread across the room, stared at Okwaho expectantly.

'That's what we're about to find out,' said A.G., his eyes never leaving their new acquaintance's face. 'Okwaho, we need answers.'

'And we'll give you some as well,' offered Aylmer. 'Sorcerer to sorcerer.'

'How long have you known you had magic?' Okwaho asked.

Aylmer hesitated. 'Since tonight.'

Okwaho scowled. 'That's impossible! It took me months to learn to use magic properly. I've been aware of mine for at least five years now.'

'Five!' exclaimed Aylmer.

'Okwaho,' began A.G., 'do you . . . have memories of your past life?' Okwaho carefully shook his head. 'Have you ever had memories that were jumbled, as though something different had occurred in another life?' Again, Okwaho shook his head, wondering what A.G. was alluding to.

'Just ask him straight,' sighed the same darker-skinned man from earlier. 'Are you a reincarnation?'

That was a loaded question if ever he'd heard one.

'Gad,' A.G. warned. He turned to Okwaho. 'Why would Moe be after you?'

'Wait, can we go back to asking me about past lives and reincarnation? Because that seemed pretty significant to me.'

The group stared at each other. It was the sole woman who broke the awkward silence.

'We all existed many centuries ago, together,' she began calmly, 'and tonight, when magic returned to Aylmer, our former lives flashed in our minds. We all know who each of us is – or was – and we also know the identities of anyone we knew then whom we know now, even if they were not present for the . . . anomaly. We know those in our lives today who were once allies or enemies, almost as though we have been given a second chance.'

She paused briefly as Okwaho took that in.

'Except you are new to us,' she went on. 'We did not know you then, and we do not know who you are or your significance, nor do we know why we have returned to this new life or why we've only now just remembered.'

Her voice was soothing; the sound eased Okwaho's tension. He nodded his gratitude. 'That is quite the experience for you all. As far as I know, I have not existed before – not in a life linked to yours or one that bears any significance to the circumstances I face in this life now.' Okwaho paused. 'Who were you, then, to all know each other again?'

'Perhaps you can first tell us more about what happened and why Moe is after you,' suggested Aylmer.

'Well, it isn't Moe who's after me. You think that kid runs that outfit?!' Okwaho scoffed. 'You're fools to think there isn't anyone above him calling the shots.'

'Morgan,' muttered A.G.

'Who?'

'His mother, my half-sister.'

'No, I've never seen that woman.' Okwaho scowled. 'I'm talking about the true leader of the biker gang, Sean.'

Everyone echoed the name in both questions and exclamations.

'Sean is a sorcerer – a powerful one. When I first started using my powers, he came to me, offered me mentorship, and for a time, I learnt under him . . . until I realised his end goal.

'He's a middle-aged man who wishes to bring people under his thumb. He's after ancient relics of legend to enhance his powers. He's been after me for many years. Tonight, my magic was subdued with a poison I know he concocted. I don't know the full extent of its effects; I just know he wishes to eliminate me as his threat.'

'He didn't kill you,' Lance observed.

'No, and the significance of that should not go unnoticed. He does not act without purpose.'

The others exchanged wary looks.

'Moe is a sorcerer,' A.G. said, his voice low. 'I don't know if Moe remembers his past life, or if he uses magic yet or not, but do you think Sean knows who Moe once was?'

'It's hard to tell, but he certainly detects his magic and probably wishes to train him.' Okwaho stared at his arm as he voiced his next thought. 'Either this was a test for Moe or he wished to have me weakened, either to destroy me more easily or in hopes I came crawling back to him to join him anew.'

'This is why we've returned,' said Gad with a look of realisation, his hands presenting the air before him. 'Yes, Moe was born after us, but we've been given a second chance to protect the people.'

'It's strange, though . . . we're so far from Ca-a-aerleon in Wales – a whole ocean away,' a man with long blond hair remarked.

'And our return also spelled Moe's return,' voiced another of the umber men, the handsome one with the tattoos on his arms.

'That just tells us how dangerous Sean is,' Casey said.

'Or we've been returned because magic has returned,' mused Aylmer. He began spitting out information in rapid-fire, bringing his hands up and fingers together as though he was seeing it all in his mind's eye. 'My arcane knowledge is limited to what I once knew, but if we assume each particle is capable of existing in space and time with its own pockets of antimatter, black holes, then, exist also within everything, at microscopic levels.'

Aylmer pointed at whatever he saw in the air, his hands dancing and moving like an orchestra conductor's, his speech never slowing.

'Quantum physics has been exploring this and other concepts, "quantum magic" being the name for such occurrences that cannot be recreated with non-quantum computers. If such a phenomenon has occurred, it might create a being capable of manipulating space-time – sorcerers, wielders of elemental and arcane magic, come to mind.'

The sorcerer refocused on the group, pushing his glasses up with his index finger. 'If one is too powerful, he could in essence become a walking black hole. That's why nature – as quantum science assumes it – would counterbalance this. Thus, our reincarnated births follow this man's birth.'

Aylmer inhaled deeply. Okwahho merely blinked at him.

'And the digestible version of this is . . . ?' A.G. prompted.

'A quantum phenomenon created Sean. Nature wished to balance that out and thus created us, including Okwaho.'

Gad scratched his chin. 'What happens if this walking black hole . . . does its whole suckage thing?'

Aylmer took a single step forward, his expression becoming more sombre and his tone more grave.

'The effects of a black hole's gravity and pressure – combined with the devouring and absorbing effects of entropic magic – instead of causing spaghettification, would make everything fold in on itself and collapse.' He swallowed loudly, his throat bobbing. 'In other words, it would cause implosion. And the more powerful this sorcerer becomes, the more destruction and carnage there will be.'

Aylmer dropped his gaze to his feet. His words came uncharacteristically slowly. 'I don't need to tell you that times are dire. It . . . is a lot to take in, even for me, and . . .' He brought a hand to his face and closed his eyes. 'I am unable to see the answers I seek to make sense of it all.'

'What does your ancient knowledge tell you?' Okwaho asked.

'That after years spent dormant,' replied Aylmer, 'magic and the arcane have returned. It is up to us, then, to ensure that balance is respected' – his tone grew more frantic, finding its usual timbre – 'else this Sean guy could very well become an entropic walking black hole.' Seeing the gaping faces of his friends, he added, 'I'm not kidding,' as they exchanged sceptical glances.

'I believe you.' A.G. passed a hand over his face. 'And Sean is training Moe. Once they become aware of who we are . . .' He trailed off, his voice heavy. Lance took his hand; Gad looked over at them gravely.

The one missing a hand stood. 'We'll do whatever you need us to.' He gazed directly at A.G. 'Courage and strength.'

'And truth above all,' another joined him.

One by one, they all stood and formed a circle, then they knelt on one knee – all but A.G.

Okwaho felt compelled to bow as well. He observed the group more carefully as he did, recalling some of their many names. After a moment, he rose.

'Your Majesty.' A.G. turned to him. Okwaho nodded. 'Now I understand who you are, as I understand your reluctance to tell me. Should Sean learn of your existence before we are ready to face him . . .' He sighed. 'Yet I am not afraid to face my former master any longer.'

Okwaho bowed regally and chanted an oath in his native language. When he rose, he met the reincarnated King's gaze. 'You have my allegiance, King Arthur Pendragon.'

'Thank you,' A.G. breathed. They shook hands, first a single firm shake, and then A.G. moved his hand up to clasp Okwaho's forearm. Matching A.G.'s smile of pride, Okwaho stood taller and reciprocated, gripping the reincarnated King's arm. A.G. nodded, and Okwaho sensed the power emanating from him.

As the two of them stepped back from each other, Okwaho cast his eyes on each of the knights, regarding them with newfound awe and appreciation.

The others began to confer, and several of them proposed reconvening in the morning after getting some rest.

Casey suggested Okwaho stay at his place where it was safe, and Devon chose to join them, wishing to monitor the wound. Several others offered to stay as well before plans were made for their next steps.

'We're still processing,' Aylmer told Okwaho. 'Once Moe remembers himself, he's going to go after A.G. all over again. We're a strong group, but we need to stay together to defeat this new threat. Sounds like the world needs us.'

'There were hundreds of Knights of the Round Table, though, no?' asked Okwaho. 'Could you not find them all?'

'We don't know if they've *all* been reincarnated,' explained Aylmer, 'but there's a reason *we* were and know each other.'

'Some are alive,' said Percy as Lamar whispered to him. 'If we help them remember, I'm sure our dad and brothers will be happy to join the new fight.'

'As will our father,' said Casey.

'You mentioned magical artefacts Sean's going after,' said Lamar as he unfolded a sleeping bag, claiming one of the couches for himself. He tossed a pillow to Bedford, who reclined in the plush chaise.

'Yes. He seeks anything that may or may not have been truly magical.' Okwaho turned to A.G. 'A while back, I know he was searching for your sword, though he has not yet found it.'

'Excalibur,' A.G. whispered. He took a deep breath and extended his hand to Okwaho, who shook it once more. 'Listen, thanks. I know we can trust you, and I hope you feel the same about us.'

'I was suspicious at first,' admitted Aylmer, 'but I can sense your verity and integrity.'

'I'd like to offer you a seat at our table – well, figuratively speaking. Welcome to the Round Table.'

Okwaho beamed, at last feeling relieved.

* * *

A.G. stood in the hall of his apartment, looking back and forth between both bedrooms. He was unsure which would be best to turn into an office, or perhaps a meditation room, or maybe a dojo. He realised he was muttering these thoughts aloud as Lance came to stand beside him.

'Which of our rooms you reckon is the biggest, Lance? Perhaps we could turn mine into the master bedroom.'

'A.G.?' sighed Lance.

'No? Would you prefer we use yours? As long as we move into the same room and spend our nights together. I'd like that.' A.G. realised this would be their first real night together in the same bed as official boyfriends.

'A.G., you're doing it again. Running away.'

'Too soon?' A blush spread across his cheeks. 'You're not ready for us to be more official?'

'I'm ready and committed, A.G.,' Lance reassured in an assertive tone, cupping A.G.'s cheek. 'We should have done this a long time ago. But you're avoiding the elephant in the room.'

A.G. looked down at his feet. He was embarrassed to admit . . . 'I'm scared.'

He heard Lance swallow. 'I'm scared, too.'

Something inside A.G. ignited, twisting his stomach in knots. He met his lover's gaze. 'You need to reconcile with Gad.'

Lance nodded. A.G. brought a hand to his head and let out a shaking breath. He moved to sit on the edge of his bed and Lance joined him, interlacing their fingers. His hand was warm, his touch comforting.

'I reckon your mattress is more comfortable,' Lance offered, 'though I guess I'll only know after spending the night with you.'

At his boyfriend's soothing tone, A.G. felt a sweet pang in his chest. He sighed. 'It's just so much to process, so much . . . to . . .' He didn't know how to put it into words.

'Maybe so. But you don't have to shoulder this alone.'

Somehow, a weight was lifted. A.G. closed his eyes and leaned into Lance, who tenderly wrapped his arms around him, holding him close until morning.

<u>Chapter Four</u>

The following morning was crisp and cloudy, and as A.G. and Lance stepped out together, their breaths misted the air in front of them. They met up with Aylmer – who was, as per his King's orders, accompanied by Gad – and together, they headed to the resto-bar before it opened for brunch.

'Why did *he* have to come with us again?' Gad complained.

'A.G. wanted me here with him,' replied Lance, turning to walk backwards to look at Gad. 'You know, 'cause I'm his boyfriend?'

Aylmer shared a sideways glance with A.G. Of course, *he* knew A.G. had invited both friends to try to help them reconcile.

'I mean, I get you'd want *one* of us,' Gad went on, ignoring Lance, 'but both of us is most assuredly unnecessary.'

'So you're just going to ignore me?' Lance spread out his arms, incredulous.

'You were right, Aylmer, it *is* quite nippy today. Glad I took your advice and wore a hat.'

'Gad!' Lance stopped right in front of Gad, forcing him to stop lest they collide. 'Just . . . tell me how you feel.'

'Furious, hurt, enraged, resentful – how do you *think* I feel?' He jutted his neck out. 'My best friend got two of my brothers killed!'

'In our past lives! A tactical miscalculation, for which I was regretful till the day Lancelot died. Gad,' Lance pleaded, looking into his eyes. 'You're my best friend. We've been given a second chance. I'm sorry. What can I do in this life to atone for my mistake from the last?'

Gad seemed to ponder before he walked around Lance. 'You can start by staying out of my way.'

Aylmer leaned towards A.G. and whispered as they all resumed, 'I think it was too soon to push for a reconciliation.'

'Wait, *that's* what this is?' Lance reached a hand towards A.G. as he caught up, looking touched. 'Baby . . .'

'Wait,' Aylmer interjected, amused. 'Baby?' He let out a laugh.

'What? What else am I supposed to call my boyfriend? We're in the twenty-first century.' Lance stuck out his neck, eyes wide.

'Yes, but . . . you're calling a king's reincarnation "baby."'

'So what, is he supposed to call him *darling*? Or better yet, *beloved!*' Gad teased Aylmer. A.G. gave Aylmer a hopeful glance.

'Sweetheart, sweety, bae?' Aylmer pondered.

'Bae?! What do you call Gen?' demanded Lance.

'Now *that* is between me and her,' replied Aylmer, pushing through the door to enter the bar. The other three let out a loud 'Woh-ho!' in response.

Immediately, Vivian came to greet them. 'What can I do for y'all?'

'There's something we need to speak to you about,' said Aylmer.

'I'm all ears, boys.'

'We need your help,' said A.G.

'Just . . . don't . . . trap me, please,' voiced Aylmer.

Vivian put a hand on her hip. 'That was *one* time, and a complete accident! Nowadays I always check the washrooms before locking 'em up at night, just in case some late-night straggler's doin' his potty business in there.'

Behind him, Gad snickered and Lance snorted a laugh. Aylmer pinched the bridge of his nose, bowing his head to hide the wave of embarrassment washing over him. '*Not* what I was referring to. *¡Me da tanta vergüenzo solo de acordarme!*'

'Is there someplace we can speak in private?' A.G. asked cautiously.

'Can do!' Vivian led them towards the back of the bar. 'Charles, I'm takin' mah break!'

She led them into the employee break room, where someone was finishing eating. After they got up and left, A.G. gave Gad and Lance a look, and the two moved to guard the door on either side.

Vivian scowled. 'What's this all about, boys?'

'You might want to sit down for this one,' A.G. suggested.

Aylmer held out his hand. 'May I take your hand, please?'

'Ooh, you gonna read my fortune?' Vivian offered him her hand, palm up.

'Something like that.' Aylmer placed his hand on Vivian's, focusing on his magic. He felt a surge of energy flow like a current from his hand to hers as a spark of light flickered for just a moment.

Vivian gasped. 'Holy fucking Grail!'

Aylmer smiled.

'Welcome back, milady,' said A.G.

'How long did y'all know you were reincarnations?' she asked, eyes wide.

A.G. filled her in as briefly as possible. 'So now we're hoping to find Excalibur before Sean does.'

'Leave it to me. I'll meditate and figure out where to look. I'll let you know what I find as soon as I've found it.'

'Thank you.' A.G. gave her his number, and Vivian stood.

'Y'all sure are lucky I moved up here from the Carolinas to live with my siblings and their spouses.'

Aylmer hesitated. 'So, about not trapping me . . .'

'Oh, you poor thing! You ain't got nothing to worry about.' Vivian pinched Aylmer's cheek. 'But only 'cause your reincarnation's so damn handsome.'

* * *

The four men strode along the sidewalk, heading back the way they'd come. 'Ooh, she has a crush on you, Aylmer,' teased Lance.

'Stop it, she's far older than my age range of interest. Plus I've got a girlfriend.'

'Maybe,' said Gad, 'but for a woman in her fifties, *she is fit!* And now she knows who we are.'

'If you're so keen,' Aylmer teased, 'why don't *you* go have your fun with her, Gad? I'm sure the Lady of the Lake's reincarnation would love to have a tryst with *Sir Gawain of the Round Table.'*

'I just might.' Gad flashed Aylmer a smirk, purposefully fixing his collar. They laughed.

'Something sure is funny,' a haughty voice announced as the speaker approached, appraising them condescendingly. Dressed head to toe in designer clothes, Morgan looked down her nose at them, scrutinising.

'Aylmer,' said A.G. He motioned his head towards Morgan. 'Show her.'

Lance pulled A.G. aside and hissed, 'Have you lost your mind? Is it wise for her to know?'

'She has a right to know. She has a chance to atone,' A.G. insisted.

Aylmer nodded. Better she learn it from them than from Sean, he reasoned. The group turned their attention back to Morgan as she eyed them curiously.

'May I take your hand?' Aylmer offered his. Morgan scrunched her nose in response, folding her arms. 'I assure you mine are clean.'

'Very well.' Sighing, Morgan placed a well-manicured hand on Aylmr's open palm. Aylmer proceeded in the same way he had with Vivian. When all was done, Morgan retracted her hand.

'And what do you expect from me now?' she demanded.

'Your son is helping a remarkably dangerous man, Morgan,' A.G. warned her. 'A sorcerer.'

Morgan pointed at Aylmer in a silent counter-argument.

'You have the chance to be on the side of good.'

'Hah!' she laughed mirthlessly. 'And you think your-self a saint? You may have been a benevolent king vying for peace between lands, A.G., but you still got more blood on your hands than I ever did.' With a scoff, Morgan turned on her heels and strutted away, her high heels clicking on the pavement.

'That could have gone better,' sighed A.G.

'It could have gone worse,' Aylmer pointed out.

* * *

Okwaho winced as feeling gradually began to return to his arm. Devon was checking his wound again and reassuring their new ally.

'Couldn't your Merlin friend heal me?' asked Okwaho.

'Doesn't quite work that way. He's still training,' replied Devon.

Okwaho chuckled. 'Yet he's the reincarnation of a legendary sorcerer.'

'Eh, what do you want?' Bedford said casually, waving a hand dismissively as he came to sit beside Okwaho.

In the apartment kitchen, Casey and Lamar were preparing food. The others had all gone home.

'Can I ask the story behind that?' Okwaho asked Bedford, pointing at his stump. 'In this life, I mean. If that's okay.'

'Nothing as heroic as losing my hand in battle while saving my brethren,' replied Bedford, a lopsided grin playing on his lips. He sobered. 'It was a driving accident. A large truck lost control and toppled onto my car before I even had time to swerve. I was stuck.' He lifted his wrist.

'I'm sorry. Must've been beyond repair.'

'Actually, no. There were two guys getting me out. One was cutting away at the metal, but the truck started to leak and a fire sparked. We had mere seconds. It was either my hand or my life.' Bedford bowed his head, staring at his stump. 'The guy who cut me free didn't make it.'

Okwaho felt a pang of sorrow. It always hurt to hear about death.

'The guy who pulled me out shielded me from the blast. He'll forever have burn scars on his back.'

Lamar came and sat down on Bedford's other side, placing a hand on his wrist. Bedford continued. 'The guy in the truck was long gone – left the scene. Wasn't even the owner. The truck had been reported missing that very morning.'

Bedford looked at Lamar. 'I've got the best roomie in the world, though, who helped me through the worst of it. I've got prosthetics at home, but I have no fear of showing my stump in public. It's a reminder of the sacrifice made to save my life that day.' He smirked. 'And besides, I hear new technologies are being used to develop some pretty nifty prosthetics. Might just have to save up and get me one of them. Might use them to dazzle the ladies.'

He winked at Lamar, placing his only hand on top of his friend's and patting it.

Okwaho glanced at his stitched arm, feeling like an idiot for worrying about his temporarily subdued magic. He looked back at Bedford. 'I think you're very brave. You survived such a . . .' He trailed off.

'Thanks. All in all, we're all brave. We're going to be fighting to protect the world from evil . . . *again.*' Bedford smiled at Okwaho.

As Casey started laying out food, Lamar stood and motioned for them to follow him to the table. The door barged open just as they were about to sit, and in marched A.G., Aylmer, Gad, and Lance.

'We were *not* getting along!' argued Gad.

'¡*Ay, Dios!* The two of you were totally getting along just now!'

Gad looked at Lance. 'Were we getting along?' Lance shrugged. 'See, he doesn't even know. He'd know for certain we were getting along *had* we been getting along, *which we were not!*' Gad concluded pointedly.

'Fine!' Aylmer sighed, exasperated. 'You weren't getting along.'

'Thank you.'

'But you both agreed,' began A.G., 'that letting Morgan remember—'

'You let Morgan remember?!' the other knights exclaimed in unison.

'—wasn't the *best* idea I've ever had.'

'Just because we agree on something doesn't mean we were getting along, it doesn't mean I'm any less angry at him, and it certainly doesn't mean I've forgiven him!'

An awkward silence fell over the group.

'So you told your sister,' Casey said, unfazed, beckoning everyone to the table. 'Care to fill us in?'

* * *

Morgan sat at their dining room table, playing with her nails. She had worked hard to build a life for herself and her son, raising him alone as best she could and rising to the top of the company as a designer to afford the luxuries she could now enjoy. And yet, the memories that had flashed in her mind – the things Aylmer showed her and the things A.G. told her – were unnerving.

Moe plopped himself down across from her. He smelled like cigarette smoke again, wearing his leather jacket and smirking like he was king of the castle. The thought made her laugh.

'What's funny, Mom?'

'Oh, just that I was lectured by that uncle of yours.'

'*Half*-uncle. And I don't consider him family.'

'You came home late last night.' She tried to sound casual, but in truth, she was worried.

'Oh, so it's my turn to be lectured?'

'I just want to know what you're up to, as your mother, so I can defend you the next time your half-uncle catches me off guard with information about you that I'm not aware of.'

Moe grinned. 'You're the best, Mom.' He leaned back, relaxing in his chair. 'Last night, ah, I was with the boys.'

'Was this . . . Sean with you?' Morgan asked, observing him carefully.

'How do you know about Sean?' His mother inclined her head. Moe scowled. 'How does *he* know about Sean?'

Morgan shrugged. 'Is he your mentor?'

'Yeah, you could call him that. He's the best. Says I'm his protégé – that's why I'm the leader, even if I'm so young.'

'The leader after *him?*'

'Yeah.' Moe crossed his arms. 'He's like a dad, okay! He's good people. You'd get along with him,' he added, a knowing glint in his eyes.

She huffed, raising an eyebrow. 'I don't need you matching me up with your friends.'

'Oh, but Mom, I think you're totally his type!'

Morgan paused. It warmed her heart, despite their emotional distance, that they could still share such moments. But if Sean was a sorcerer, of course she'd be his type.

'Last night, Sean was with you, yes?' she pressed.

'No, he went on a trip. He left me in charge.'

'And what does he show you when he's in charge?'

'Just stuff.' Moe shrugged. 'How to be a real man, stuff like that.'

'I see.'

Morgan left the matter at that as Moe went on about his exploits biking over steep hills with his friends.

'You should've seen me! I was going down at almost a ninety-degree angle . . .'

* * *

A.G. looked down at his phone as Vivian's message illuminated the screen, excitement filling his entire being. Lance laced his hand with his, caressing A.G.'s leg under the table and kissing him on the cheek. The affectionate gesture sent a tingle straight to A.G.'s stomach, almost making him forget himself in his sudden desire for more of his boyfriend.

'Your brother looks like he's *this* close to telling you it's rude to scroll on your phone at the table,' Lance murmured. Why was his voice so seductive when A.G. wanted to focus?

'Because it is,' Casey said matter-of-factly.

A.G.'s heart stammered before realising what Casey was referring to. With a deep breath, he steadied himself.

'It's Vivian. She's found Excalibur!' A.G. looked up. Everyone's eyes were wide as they stared at him expectantly. 'Boys, we're booking a trip overseas . . .' He turned his phone around, displaying the link Vivian had sent him. 'To the Arthurian Museum of Wales.'

CHAPTER FIVE

A.G., Lance, Gad, Aylmer, and Okwaho stood before a pane of glass encasing a large stone with a sword in its centre. The other knights had fanned out strategically throughout the museum – those who had accompanied them, at least. Lance held A.G.'s hand, which would have been comforting if not for the item right in front of him.

'This isn't Excalibur,' said A.G., dismayed. 'We flew all the way here for nothing.'

'Not nothing,' stated Okwaho. '*He's* here. I can sense him.'

'The real Excalibur has to be here *some*where,' Aylmer agreed.

'But this *is* the real Excalibur,' a museum employee insisted as he ambled up to the group. He reeked of cologne, his stiff hair had far too much gel, and he looked like he was about to recite whatever drivel he had memorised about A.G.'s past life as though he knew better. A.G. knew his type.

He slowly turned to the young employee, trying not to drip annoyance. 'Where is Excalibur?'

'Why, right here,' the employee replied with that mastered smile. He sounded exactly like the type A.G. judged him to be.

'This isn't Excalibur.'

'And how would *you* know?' the employee condescended. 'I have studied Arthurian legends since I started working here,' he drawled. 'Did you know . . . that King Arthur—'

A.G. held up a finger, interrupting the employee before he could further confirm A.G.'s assessment. He fought the urge to roll his eyes.

'This gem, here, is supposed to be chipped. And don't get me started on the way the light reflects off it. Excalibur was a well-balanced sword . . . *for its owner –* thus, it was just that slightly off-balance when held on the open palm of a hand. Only in Arthur Pendragon's hand did it balance perfectly.'

The employee blinked. Gad nudged A.G. with his elbow, tipping his head towards a hooded figure going into a back room. Without thinking twice, A.G. dashed after the mysterious person, his friends calling for him to wait.

'Hey, you're not allowed to run!' the employee shouted. 'Hey! You're not allowed back there!'

A.G. pushed open a heavy door and emerged into a room where many relics sat, also secured in glass cases. And there, where the hooded figure hovered, in real stone – Excalibur.

It felt like it was calling out to A.G. Wasting no time, the reincarnated King ran forward and kicked the figure away from the glass case.

'Step away from the sword.'

The figure's hood flew back to reveal a man in his mid-forties, his dark hair just a bit lighter with some grey, a stern expression on his face, his build strong. The others rushed into the room and the man's attention went to Okwaho. He sneered, lifting his hand.

'I don't think so,' said Aylmer, firing a spell that shoved him further away.

'So you've found friends to protect you, Okwaho. Well, they'll fail,' the stranger condescended.

Lance leaned towards the Mohawk and murmured, 'Is this him?'

'Yes,' Okwaho confirmed, glaring at his former master. 'This is Sean.'

The older sorcerer sneered at Aylmer. 'The magic this young man possesses is too ancient to match mine! I don't know who taught you, chap, but—'

Aylmer cast another spell to shut him up, cyan magic swirling around Sean and making him stagger as he cast a counterspell to absorb it.

A.G. kicked at the glass to no avail.

'These must be bulletproof,' said Gad.

Aylmer and Okwaho were busy with Sean, exchanging colourful spells. From the looks of it, Okwaho's magic could still do some damage, making A.G. wonder how powerful he was when it wasn't subdued.

Despite their focus on the older man, the Chilean sorcerer spun and aimed a spell at the glass casing before turning back around to send Sean a fireball. The glass shattered as the magic met its target and Excalibur rang, calling out to its master.

Lance blocked Sean's arm, trying to keep him busy, but the older man lifted Lance by the throat, choking him, and flung him against the wall. His body crumpled as it hit the floor.

'Focus,' Gad advised. A.G. realised he was staring at Lance, poised to join the fight. Steeling himself, he returned his attention to his sword.

Gad yelped as Sean pulled him away. Lance rushed to him and blocked the strong blow before Gad blocked a hit that would have knocked Lance out. The two exchanged a quick sheepish smile before nodding and coordinating an attack, using their arms as though they were daggers to keep Sean away from A.G., whose attention kept being split.

A.G. felt his sword singing to him. He gripped the hilt with both hands – it felt like coming home.

'That won't work!' snarled Sean. 'That sword was solidly encased in that stone by powerful magic.'

'Yeah,' agreed Aylmer, 'it was placed there by Merlin himself.'

'Only someone with equally powerful magic can pull it out.'

'Or the sword's rightful owner!' declared A.G.

He took a breath and heaved, the sword only resisting enough to ensure A.G.'s intent was clear. As he retrieved the sword from its stone, its ringing echoed through the room, singing the song A.G. now remembered from his life once lived long ago.

He lifted the sword above his head, holding it towards the ceiling with one hand. The grip, the weight – it felt so familiar. In this life, he'd never held a sword, but now it was as though he knew all he once had.

'How?' Sean demanded with a growl, sending out a shockwave that shook the room and stunned the others in place. Yet A.G. never faltered in the face of this sorcerer's might, emboldened by Excalibur. 'Are you a Pendragon heir?'

'No.' A.G. pointed the sword at Sean, its tip mere inches away from his chest. 'I am the reincarnation of Arthur Pendragon himself. I am this sword's rightful owner.' As if to emphasise his point, the sword gleamed with an ethereal glow.

Sean laughed sinisterly. 'Bold of you to reveal yourself to me, *and* assume you can still stop me.'

'What is your goal, Sean? What's the purpose of all this?'

'Now *that* would be telling.'

Sean abruptly lifted his arms, conjuring a gust of wind that sent Gad, Okwaho, and Aylmer flying out of the room. A.G. was flung against the wall, nearly dropping his sword.

Sean cast a spell of dark light, and Excalibur coruscated. A.G. instinctively lifted the blade, angling it in a two-handed grip, flat side facing Sean, to block the spell.

'A.G.!' cried Lance, hesitating between action and watching the sword work its fabled magic to protect its King.

Sean continued pushing against A.G. as he struggled to maintain the parry, yet somehow the light reflected away from the sword, creating a small barrier that protected A.G. from the evil magic. A.G. then pushed forward, holding his position.

'Lance, get out of here!' The magic against the sword grew brighter, sizzling with lighting.

'I can't leave you!'

'Go, Lance, go!' A.G. shouted. Lance gaped at him, fear in his eyes. 'Damnit, Lance! Just get out of here!'

'No!' cried Lance, desperation in his voice.

Struggling against the building magic with sweat dripping down his face, barely seeing the satisfied sneer on Sean's features, A.G. turned his head to Lance. 'Excalibur will protect me,' he said, his voice low, calm.

Reluctantly, Lance backed away before hurrying out of the room.

Commanding his sword, A.G. shouted, 'Now!' and pushed as hard as he could.

The magic exploded around him, sending Sean staggering backwards towards the far wall. The light was blinding, and a pulse of what felt like electricity vibrated up A.G.'s arms. He heard Sean hiss a complaint.

The younger man turned and darted out of the room, shouting to the others, 'Go, go, go!'

* * *

The scattered knights made for the various exits as security officers hurried after them.

Lamar pushed past a door, listening for footsteps. Bedford pointed at a shadow ahead. 'There!'

Percy sprinted forward as the group of men ran to catch up with a fleeing Sean. Casey, Raven, and Gallagher broke off down an alley while Lamar, Bedford, and Boris continued straight ahead. Sean veered into another alleyway, followed by one group. The other three came running up the side alley, boxing Sean in between the six of them.

'You're cornered, Sean,' stated Casey.

'Or am I?'

Sean jumped into the air, grabbing onto a low emergency staircase and lifting himself up. Boris leapt and grabbed the man by the legs, pulling him back down, and Sean kicked Boris off him once they reached the ground.

'I am warning you . . .'

As the knights closed in around him, Sean turned to look at one of them, then spun back to look at another.

'You lot don't have magic. I do.'

'It didn't stop us in our previous lives,' declared Raven, taking a step forward. 'It won't stop us now.'

Sean laughed, a sinister sound. 'You play a dangerous game. The more you push me, the more I am tempted to cause more carnage.' He smirked and lowered his tone. 'I thrive on the suffering of others.'

'Then we'll ensure there is no suffering so your powers cannot grow,' declared Casey.

Sean narrowed his eyes as they landed on Bedford. The laugh that followed was a hideous declaration that sent a shiver down Lamar's spine.

'Well, what do you know?' Sean reached into his pocket and pulled out a keychain. He began removing the keys. 'I've kept this all these years. I suppose you should have a memento of your survival.'

He tossed the empty keychain to Bedford, who caught it with his only hand. He stared down at it, his jaw tight.

'Bedford?' Lamar asked gently.

'This is the logo that was on that truck.' Bedford seethed at Sean, 'It was *you*, the driver who caused the accident. Who caused this.' Bedford lifted his stump. Sean merely laughed, amused. 'A man died that day!'

'And my powers grew stronger.' Sean smirked.

Bedford lunged forward, poised to strike the man, but Sean was quick with a spell that sent all six knights flailing backwards. Bedford clutched his stump and fell to his knees, crying out hoarsely – a wail of terror Lamar had only heard from him when he used to have nightmares about the accident.

Sean darted away and rounded a corner before anyone could give pursuit.

Lamar could only think of his roommate as he rushed to him and cradled him in his arms. 'He's gone . . . I've got you.'

Bedford grew quiet.

Then, 'I don't know what he did, but it felt like it was happening all over again.'

Overcome with rage, Bedford rose and balled his hand into a fist. Lamar placed a gentle hand on his friend's shoulder. Instantly, Bedford deflated and bowed his head, trembling the way he would shortly after the accident happened.

Lamar had his arms around him again, stroking his back, repeating the same comforting words he would once tell him again and again. The others joined the hug, just as they would whenever Bedford had flashbacks. It was a ritual that had become second nature to them all.

A moment later, Bedford backed away, closed his eyes, and took a deep breath. 'Okay. I'm good.'

'It's okay to relive things, Bedford. That guy nearly killed you.'

'Lamar, he's going to kill us *all* if we don't stop him!'

'That's why we're out here,' said Raven. 'Let's go make sure A.G. and the others don't encounter Sean so we can take Excalibur home.'

Bedford nodded, looking down at the keychain. 'You're right. Let's regroup and plan our next step.'

* * *

A.G. slammed open a door to a stairwell and bounded down, skipping two steps at a time.

'What the hell happened in there?!' demanded Aylmer.

'No time. I'll explain later,' A.G. answered quickly.

He kicked open an exit door and ran out into an alley. Lance grabbed his arm, pulling him back, his eyes frantic and jaw set. He was breathing heavily. Seeing the worry on his face, A.G. felt a pang of guilt and hoped Lance would sense his apology. A.G. cupped his lover's cheek, taking a moment to catch his breath.

Before he could say anything, a team of armed troops ran into the alley, weapons trained on the five escapees. Turning to face the guards, A.G. lifted his arms in surrender yet maintained his grip, unwilling to let Excalibur go.

CHAPTER SIX

The tall woman leading the troops took several steps forward. She looked to be in her early thirties, with a strong build, ash-blonde hair tied into a bun, and blue eyes as vivid as they were frightening. Her scowl sent shivers down Lance's back.

'Drop the sword!' she commanded. A.G. didn't move. She laughed mirthlessly. 'You think you're the first wannabe I've dealt with? I lead the division specifically for Arthurian artefacts.'

'Maybe,' said A.G., 'but this sword doesn't belong to you.'

This time, the laugh that escaped her was spontaneous. 'Fancy yourself an Arthur Pendragon heir, do you?' Her Welsh accent was thick. 'You're not even Welsh, or British at best.'

'I'm Canadian. So?'

'A.G.?' Lance whispered in warning.

'Listen, ma'am,' began Aylmer, 'we're not the ones you should be worrying about.'

'I'll be the judge of that.' She took several steps forward. 'Now, I'll ask you again, but only once more – *drop. The sword.*'

'Look, this sword belongs to me, and I can prove it,' A.G. explained.

'Oh, pulled it out of the stone, did you? Well, I've got news for you: it's a fake. So why don't you just return my property,' she condescended, 'and I'll let you go back to Canada.'

'A fake, you say?' A.G. lifted Excalibur vertically, keeping its point towards the ground. 'Not this one!' As if in response, Excalibur glinted, a light travelling from its hilt to its tip.

The woman's eyes widened. 'Squad, stand down.'

She stared at A.G. for a long moment before she spoke again. Everyone else remained perfectly still, not daring to move or speak.

'Arthur Pendragon had no heir, for he had no sons.' She paused deliberately. 'What the stories omit is that it doesn't mean he was childless.'

'That's correct,' said A.G. 'He had a daughter.'

Lance observed the woman. Ever since their past lives had been revealed to them, they knew or at least recognised those they'd known in their former lives. This woman was not a reincarnation.

'How do you know that?' Lance asked her.

'Arthur Pendragon is my ancestor.'

She placed her palm on the flat of the sword and it reacted to her touch, shimmering with magic. A.G. gasped and mimicked her gesture.

Immediately, the sword pulsed and vibrated, the pair lifting several feet into the air as magic flowed between them. They gaped at each other, unmoving in their magical lift.

Aylmer bent his knees, curling his fingers in a ready stance while Okwaho held out both hands in preparation. Lance glanced at Gad, who moved to flank A.G. on his other side.

The two Pendragons descended abruptly and touched the ground once more, staggering back from each other. Lance ran to A.G.'s side, steadying him by the arms.

'What happened?' cried Aylmer.

'I saw . . .' A.G. began, out of breath.

'I have been awaiting this moment since I was a child,' the woman said, marvelling at A.G. as though he held the key to all her answers.

'. . . her vision,' A.G. completed.

'It was abstract, it was vague, but one thing was clear – when the true Excalibur is removed from the stone, Arthur Pendragon has returned to protect the lands from the Arcane.'

'Whoa,' muttered Aylmer.

'That . . . tracks,' said Gad.

'I . . .' It was A.G.'s turn to marvel at her and the vision he'd just seen.

While the group began to process this, the others came running into the alley, out of breath and ranting about Sean.

'Right. Let's speak somewhere more private.' The woman turned and issued orders to her troops, then turned back to the group. 'By the way, I'm Serena.' She narrowed her eyes. 'Do *not* call me Rena or Seree.' Striding forward, she began to lead the group out of the alley.

'I wonder what *that's* all about,' Lance muttered. He gave Gad a hopeful glance, but Gad walked right past him.

Gad paused. 'Look, Lance, just because we helped each other back there doesn't mean I've forgiven you yet. I care about you, but . . .' He worked his jaw for a moment, then he stalked off. Lance sighed.

* * *

Aylmer lay on his back in the hotel bed, attempting to quell his shaking body. Up until now, since his initial freak-out, he'd remained relatively calm . . . too calm. Everything was starting to catch up to him, and his mind was whirling.

Gen, who dozed with an arm on his chest, suddenly stirred. She sat up to look at him. 'What's wrong?'

Aylmer couldn't even meet her gaze. Everything he wanted to promise her had just been thrown out the window – and not of his own volition.

He stood and walked over to the window, staring out.

'Aylmer?' Gen joined him a little hesitantly. He kept his back to her.

Aylmer closed his eyes, his heart beating too fast to count. 'That . . . encounter with Sean . . .' he stammered. 'It made me realise something I'd failed to grasp until now . . .' He whispered the next words. 'I might die.'

Gen wrapped her arms around him from behind.

'I failed him, Gen. I failed to protect Arthur last time. Can I truly keep A.G. alive? Sean is so powerful, I couldn't hold my own back there. He's going to turn into a literal walking black hole if we don't do something, and . . . his magic might implode me.'

Kissing Aylmer's shoulder, Gen caressed his chest in soothing strokes. The warmth from the tingle rising in him sent a pang to his clenching stomach. He gently peeled her hands off him and turned to face her.

'Gen,' he whispered, his heart breaking, 'when we get back home . . .' He swallowed. 'I think it's best we go our separate ways.'

Gen froze before taking a step back, shock and hurt on her face. The sight tormented him.

'You mean . . . break up?' All he could do was nod as his heart drummed faster. 'But I love you,' she protested in a half whisper.

Something inside Aylmer overtook him. Forgetting himself, he grabbed Gen, pressing his hand to the small of her back, and kissed her desperately, as though it was the only thing that would keep him from drowning.

He let go abruptly, backing away from her. 'Gen, I love you so much I wanted to spend the rest of my life with you. But I can't promise you that . . . not when the rest of my life might be measured in literal weeks.'

Aylmer realised there were tears streaming down his face. Gen cupped his wet cheek. Closing his eyes, Aylmer leaned into her touch. 'I . . . I even bought a ring.'

'Then why break up?' Gen asked gently. 'I'd rather spend whatever time we have left together than apart.'

'But I'm going to break your heart if I die,' insisted Aylmer, staring her in the eyes, frantic.

'And you're not breaking it now?'

That hit Aylmer right in the gut. 'Gen, up until now, I was a regular Canadian-Chilean geek. And now . . . now that my past life has caught up to me and my magic has returned . . .'

Gen's expression hardened. 'You're an idiot if you think I wouldn't say yes just because we face battle or uncertainty.'

As the invisible grip on Aylmer's heart tightened, he made up his mind. 'Then I'm an idiot. Because I don't want to lose you – I just want to protect you.' He took her hands in his. 'Gen, I want to promise you so many things, but I can't right now. I can only promise you this: that I will do my best to survive, to protect you . . . and when this is over, I want the only thing I dedicate my life to – that I *pledge* myself to – to be you.'

He took a step closer, his face a mere inch away from hers. '*Te amo.* I will ask properly when we achieve victory, but I want to also ask now. Gen, Geneviève, Guinevere . . . will you marry me?'

'Yes.' There was no hesitation.

Aylmer kissed her with the same desperation as before but now melded with determination. And as they enveloped each other, he made love to her right there by the window – a promise to be together forever, no matter how uncertain forever looked.

* * *

The group flew back to Canada the following day with Serena in tow, who used her authority and access codes to get Excalibur on the plane and through security unnoticed. Somehow, the flight felt longer than it should have. Lance kept glancing Gad's way with puppy dog eyes, and Gad couldn't decide if he was more annoyed or saddened by the situation. He didn't even know why he couldn't just let go of all his pent-up anger. He supposed the memories were still too fresh, like opening up a healing wound.

Upon their return, A.G. wanted to fill everyone in together at Casey's. Naturally, Gad appointed himself as the one to alert their Lady of the Lake waitress.

Hand on the resto-bar's door, he paused, a wave of anxiety rolling over him. He shook it off and marched in, heading straight to Vivian.

'How's my favourite waitress!' he greeted, grinning flirtatiously.

'How's my favourite knight?' She winked. 'Don't tell any of the others I called you that.'

Gad laughed nervously, feeling a rush of heat. He shook *that* off too. 'Listen, we're having a meeting tonight to put everyone in the loop and discuss our next steps. We'd like you to be there. What time do you get off work?'

'I finish at seven.'

'Great. I'll pick you up at seven fifteen!' With that settled, Gad started turning.

Vivian let out a laugh. 'Said like that, one might think you were fixin' to take me out on a date.'

Gad stopped in his tracks. Slowly, he spun back to Vivian. 'And what if I did . . . take you out on a date?'

Vivian playfully slapped his arm. 'Now you're just messin' with me!'

'I'm not.' They both grew serious. 'After tonight's meeting, how about I take you out somewhere? Just the two of us . . . as a date.'

A blush spread across Vivian's cheeks. 'You like *all* your women mature?'

'I like *you*,' Gad blurted. In reality, Gad was one of the eldest of the group in this life – he was forty. Vivian was only fifteen years older than him . . . approximately.

'All right. I accept.'

Gad beamed, his stomach somersaulting. 'Great. See you tonight!'

As he stepped out of the restaurant, he reflexively took out his phone and tapped to send Lance a message. His heart dropped as he remembered they still weren't on speaking terms. Deflated, he put his phone away.

Once they had all gathered for the meeting, with Casey's bite-sized oven snacks filling their bellies, everyone was filled in on the latest news, and plans were made. The group soon warmed to Serena, and she was happy to meet them all.

'Something still puzzles me, though,' voiced Boris. 'How is it we were all born *after* Sean, even if some of us are just a handful of years younger than he is, while Vivian is older than even him? I thought we were reincarnated because of his existence to help balance magic back out.'

'I actually have an explanation for that,' said Vivian. 'This ain't my first reincarnation rodeo. As the Lady of the Lake who once guarded Excalibur before bestowin' it upon King Arthur, I've been returning every century or so as a guardian of sorts. Not sure what my purpose was before now, but I remember all my past lives since then. I just so happen to be older than y'all, but I could have been born later, too.'

'I'm happy you're just the way you are,' Gad found himself saying before he could stop himself. He cleared his throat, looking down at his feet.

'If you're a reincarnation,' began Tristan, 'I've been musing about this in my head since the other day – that means you died. How?'

'Actually,' said Vivian, 'I'm still bound to the lake. Part of me is connected to it, and one day I have to return, else my spirit will remain split forever.'

'Could you return now? Out of curiosity . . .' asked Serena.

'Because of Sean's magic, I reckon, I can't connect to the other half of my soul. If he succeeds, I'll never return.' She scrunched up her face in confusion, shaking her head. 'It's like I split myself in two, but that split came along with some dangers. I'll need to return someday, whether in this life or the next, but I need to remember myself to do that. I need to be alive to do that, and I need a purpose fulfilled to do that.'

She shrugged, presenting her hand as though the future lay in it. 'After Sean's defeat – should we succeed, that is – I get to choose when I return and when it's the best lifetime for it. Otherwise, too many reincarnations and I may destroy myself.'

That hit Gad with a pang of worry.

'I mean, it *has* been a thousand four hundred and eighty years, just about,' voiced Boris.

Vivian rubbed her forehead. 'I just can't remember what compelled me to do such a thing in the first place, splittin' my soul in two. It's the only thing I can't remember.'

'The important thing is, we're all here and we have a plan . . . more or less,' said A.G. 'And it means a lot to me to have you all by my side once more.' He laced his fingers through Lance's and smiled warmly at them all.

As everyone dispersed, Gad and Vivian snuck out without the others noticing they were leaving together. He didn't want anyone teasing them just yet.

'It's a little late,' said Gad. 'How about I make you dinner at my place?'

'Sounds lovely.'

Those snacks had been pretty filling, so he wasn't all that hungry, but Gad wanted to spend time alone with his Lady of the Lake. He chuckled to himself – *his* Lady.

But when they reached his apartment, for some reason he wasn't able to get his key in the lock properly.

Vivian placed a hand on his. 'You're nervous,' she said, her voice gentle.

'I'm sorry, I . . . it's been a while since I've done this.' He met Vivian's gaze. Her smile was gorgeous, the lines on her face only deepening her beauty even more to him, accentuating her maturity, and his breath hitched.

'Then let me break the ice,' she whispered.

She pressed a sweet kiss to Gad's lips which they both quickly deepened. Even while fumbling to get the door unlocked and open, Gad never stopped kissing her.

Finally, he kicked the door shut behind them, wrapping his arms around Vivian. They barely made it past the entryway corridor before they were already naked.

CHAPTER SEVEN

A.G. sat with his head in his hands, thinking. 'We still don't have all the puzzle pieces.' He lifted his head and looked at his sword which lay on the long coffee table before him. Serena had provided him with a sheath, but he had left the sword out bare, hoping it would inspire him.

Lance sighed. 'Baby, you're overthinking it.' He sat down beside A.G. and rubbed his back. 'First, you try to avoid it – now you're obsessing.'

'I'm an overcompensator.'

Lance smirked cheekily. 'There are some things you do not have to compensate for.'

A.G. laughed. 'Yeah? And what's that?' He wrapped his arms around Lance, nibbling the other man's lower lip. As they kissed sweetly, A.G. felt cocooned in the warmth of their love.

The doorbell rang. A.G. groaned a complaint, his lips still on Lance's.

'They'll go away,' whispered Lance, leaning forward and pushing A.G. down onto the sofa.

The doorbell rang again. A.G. sighed.

'Let them ring the damn doorbell.' Lance reclaimed his boyfriend's lips, slipping his hands beneath his shirt. He and A.G. chuckled as they continued to make out.

Then the doorbell not only rang, but Morgan's voice echoed into the apartment as though they had pressed the buzzer's intercom.

'I want to speak with you, A.G.'

Lance paused where he'd been feeling A.G. up, his hand falling limp under the other man's shirt. The two men sighed at the same time.

'Well that certainly kills the mood,' said Lance.

'She used her magic.' Resigned, A.G. stood and buzzed Morgan up.

He sighed again – he just couldn't stop sighing now. Lance made that face that said he knew what A.G. was thinking and feeling, and it warmed his heart.

A moment later, Morgan entered the apartment. 'Thank you for letting me in.'

'Not like you gave us much choice,' muttered A.G.

'I hope I wasn't interrupting anything.'

A.G. glared at her. 'You know very well you were interrupting something.'

'Well, you're both dressed, so clearly it wasn't—' She stopped, looking as though the action required substantial effort. 'Sorry.'

A.G. blinked, taken aback. He looked at Lance, who merely shrugged and shook his head, also at a loss.

'Wait, did you just . . . ? Did you just stop yourself from deriding me? And *apologise?*'

Morgan shifted her weight. 'I've reflected on what you said. I . . . want to mend bridges.'

Now, A.G. was even more taken aback. He had known how to deal with her usual condescension, but this? This was new.

'Has something happened?' he asked.

In Morgan's eyes, there was a plea.

'How about some tea?' offered Lance.

'Thank you.' Morgan let A.G. take her coat and the three of them moved to the kitchen.

'This is . . . cosy,' Morgan said carefully, looking around the small kitchen as she sat down at the table. 'Congratulations, by the way. It was about time the two of you became an item.' Her tone was back to its usual deriding timbre, but an amused smile replaced the smirk of condescension that usually accompanied it.

'Not you too,' complained A.G. as he sat across from her, though he was pleased to hear her sentiments. Lance chuckled, joining them at the table with the steeping tea.

'I never knew what that was like, living with someone, falling in love – truly in love.'

'What about Moe's father?' inquired A.G.

'There was passion, sure, but he used me and fled the moment he learnt I was pregnant. I raised Moe alone, and now . . .' She pressed her lips together. 'I'm worried about him. He spoke about Sean – told me the man is teaching him to be a proper man.'

'Yeah, and we know what "proper man" means to Sean,' muttered A.G.

'If Sean is a dangerous sorcerer, he might use Moe, and that worries me. I don't want to lose my son, but . . . Arthur.' Morgan reached a hand towards him. 'May we begin anew?'

A.G. was so moved, he found his eyes stinging. 'Yes,' he answered softly.

Lance looked down at his lap. 'I need to fully reconcile with Gad. If the two of you can speak civilly . . . I need to plead my case. We can't let things stand as they are.'

'That is why I am here,' said Morgan. 'I know I've been a bitch to you, but this time I don't want to make the same mistakes.'

A.G. smiled warmly, taking her hand in his. 'Then let's begin anew, sister.'

Without another word, Lance bolted up and headed for the door. Morgan blinked. Lance quickly ran back and kissed A.G. on the cheek.

'Good luck, babe!' A.G. called out. Then Lance was gone.

Morgan suppressed a laugh as A.G. poured the tea. The air around them felt . . . refreshed.

* * *

Gad opened the door as Lance shivered outside.

'Gad, just hear me out, please,' Lance blurted before the man could close his door on him.

Gad folded his arms, waiting. Lance took that as his cue to continue.

'I was in the wrong. I should have checked better – that miscalculation at the time seemed like it was inevitable. I gave an order in panic, and it got your brothers killed. Had I waited but a few minutes, they might have received the warning. I honestly thought the only soldiers left were enemy soldiers. You have to believe me.'

Lance got down on his knee with a hand on his heart. 'I ask you – no, I beg of you – to please forgive me. Gad . . . no, Gawain, I am so sorry.'

Tears fell from his eyes, but he never blinked or looked away. His gaze was locked on Gad, waiting.

Gad sighed. 'Come in – you look like you're proposing, and the last thing I want is your boyfriend thinking I'm out to steal his man. Get up.' He offered him his hand. Tearfully, Lance took it and stood. He followed Gad inside, where the two men stared at each other in the small corridor.

Gad blinked back tears before a sob escaped him. 'I mourned them until I died.'

'I know,' wept Lance.

'They died, and it felt like you had sacrificed them for the greater good. But I know, had you known they were still there, you would have held off as long as you could.'

Both wept openly a few moments more.

'I'm so sorry, Gad,' Lance whispered.

'I know, Lance . . . Lancelot.' Gad bowed his head. 'I hate these feelings, and I just want my best friend back, because in this life you've always been there for me.' He met Lance's gaze. 'You stood up for me to anyone who threw racial slurs at me. We were teens, from different backgrounds, different cultures, but I always felt like you were my fourth brother.'

Lance put a hand to his mouth, still sobbing.

Gad whispered, 'I forgive you.'

And as he pulled Lance into a strong hug, holding him for a long time, both wept. When they finally pulled away, they laughed sheepishly and wiped their eyes.

'I think what made me angrier was the thought that our rift caused Arthur's death.'

'There were many factors that might have helped had they been different, but it's not our rift that killed him,' said Lance. 'We cannot know what could have been, and that detail being a contributing factor is mere speculation from historians. Heck, we're not even thought to be real!'

Gad laughed. 'This reincarnation thing is insane! Isn't it?!' He hissed out a laugh. 'I could use a cold one. You?' he asked, starting into the apartment proper.

'Yeah.' It was early, but Lance agreed with Gad.

The two sat down together and each popped open a can of beer. They took a sip in silence, the air between them still awkward.

Gad turned his head to Lance. 'You never told me what happened that morning you and A.G. became boyfriends.'

Lance blushed, feeling the tension ease.

'What about you?' Lance teased, nudging Gad with his elbow. Gad grinned, looking eager to share about his recent romantic liaison.

'You first,' said Gad. 'It happened first.'

Lance chuckled. 'All right.'

He excitedly recounted to Gad how it went down, and Gad was excited with him, asking for all the details only a best friend would care to know.

* * *

Casey pocketed his phone and turned to his two guests. 'Well, it seems Morgan wants to help us if she can.'

'That's excellent news,' Serena beamed.

'It still doesn't change that Sean wants to control Moe, though,' said Okwaho as he moved his arm about, turning his wrist. He flicked his hand open and an orb of crystalline light glowed in it. A smile crossed his face. 'It's back. My magic has returned to full capacity!' Any healing his arm might have still needed was now complete. He stood. 'There is much to do.'

'I agree. We should focus our efforts on thwarting Sean's magic,' suggested Serena.

'To start, we must learn what created Sean in the first place,' declared Okwaho.

'You were here when Aylmer explained it,' said Casey. 'The whole black hole thing.'

'Forget quantum science,' said Okwaho, '*magic* created Sean. There is no doubt in my mind about that. And if a magic more sinister and evil than Sean created him, where is it, and how do we stop it?'

* * *

Morgan sat in the living room, waiting for Moe to come home.

'Mom, I'm back!'

She stood and folded her arms as her son sauntered into the house. She had to keep herself from spouting off at him the instant he strode in. But even with her restraint, she was unable to stop the tapping of her foot.

'What's with the look?'

Morgan took a steadying breath. 'I learnt from your uncle today—'

'Half-uncle,' corrected Moe, mimicking her stance.

'—that Sean has you running around attacking people.'

Moe scowled. 'Whatever, Mom – you don't get it. The guy was coming after Sean!'

'You sliced his arm open. That's violence, Moe.'

'You want to argue about it with him, Mom? Because he's waiting outside.'

Morgan was shocked. 'You invited him here? Do you even know what he is?'

'Yeah, yeah,' Moe dismissed. 'A criminal, I get it. But I meant what I said before – you're totally his type.'

Without waiting for a reply, Moe sauntered back to the door to let Sean into the house. Morgan had to compose herself, lest her fear show on her face. She plastered on a fake smile.

The man who walked in the door was middle-aged, handsome at first glance but with dark circles around his eyes that weren't caused by fatigue. He smiled at Morgan, his eyes scanning her physique. Moe grinned knowingly.

As they stood in the living room and made small talk, Sean spoke suavely and held himself tall, flexing and showing his best attributes. Morgan tried her best to keep it casual. Moe excused himself to take a quick phone call, leaving the two of them – which she suspected he probably did on purpose.

She hesitated, and Sean's expression changed dangerously. He strode up to her and leaned in close.

'You know what you are, what your son is?' Sean asked, his voice low. The question shouldn't have surprised Morgan, but it did. 'You do, don't you?'

Morgan had considered telling Moe before tonight but hesitated, fearing it would only make things worse. However, if Sean knew . . .

'I know more than you could guess,' Morgan chose to reply.

'Considering I just had a run-in with the Knights of the Round Table, I'm guessing I know exactly *who* you are.'

Morgan's eyes widened. That was a confirmation if ever she heard one.

'So you know,' Sean smirked knowingly, 'and yet you choose to side against me.'

'I haven't chosen a side,' Morgan lied, scowling. 'My son has always come first.' That, at least, was the truth.

Sean smiled, satisfied with her answer. He was exploiting her son, but to what extent, even A.G. didn't know. No one knew except for Sean himself.

Moe returned and found Sean leaning towards his mother, hand on her arm. Morgan didn't know when Sean had grabbed her, but it frightened her that she had been so focused on his words, his voice, his face, that he had slipped through her defences.

'Should I make another phone call and come back?' asked Moe.

Sean smiled at Morgan. 'Sadly, we need to head out.' His fingers grazed her face, and a chill ran down her spine – Morgan fought the urge to shudder. 'Until we meet again, Morgan.'

Sean backed away and turned to leave, Moe right behind him. As they exited, Morgan heard Sean whisper to Moe.

'Your mother is sceptical of me. You need to get her on our side. Once you do that . . .'

The rest was lost as Moe shut the door and they departed from the house.

Fear gripping her, Morgan finally let out a shaking breath and sank down to the floor, clutching her chest.

Chapter Eight

'So that's a dozen more knights rememberin' their past selves to add to our arsenal, I reckon,' said Vivian as she slid into the booth to join those present. 'Ain't that somethin'?'

Lance was cuddled up with A.G., Aylmer was sipping a beer, and Gad had his arm over Vivian's shoulders, while Serena and Okwaho sat next to each other.

'Arsenal!' chuckled Lance.

'She's right,' said Serena. 'If Moe remembers who he is, we have a big problem – as big as Sean.'

'Now if only I could remember why I split my soul like this,' sighed Vivian.

Gad pressed a hand to her cheek, the umber a stark contrast with her pale complexion, and smiled. 'It'll come back to you in time.' As Vivian leaned into his touch, Gad had to remind himself they were in public, lest he kiss her with abandon.

'Aww, the two of you are so adorable,' voiced Lance. He and Gad, along with Vivian, seemed to be the only ones in good spirits.

Aylmer slammed the empty beer mug onto the table.

Okwaho's eyes widened. 'You downed that fast.'

'Yeah, well, you only live once . . . or in our case, twice.' A shadow crossed his face. 'I wrote my will today.'

Everyone sobered at that. Gad had never given it much thought, but he realised it might be wise they all do so, given the circumstances.

'It feels like I've been given a death sentence.' Aylmer removed his glasses and rubbed his eyes, letting out a series of expletives in Spanish.

'You must believe in your magic, Aylmer,' said Okwaho. 'You're Merlin. That counts for a lot.' Aylmer merely looked away. 'You have so much power within you, I can feel it pulsating. Magic is on your side, and that's because you are the reincarnation of Merlin.'

'Yeah, well, maybe I don't *want* to be fucking Merlin.'

Putting his glasses back on his face and grabbing his coat, Aylmer stood and stormed out of the bar.

'Should we . . . ?' began Serena.

'He needs a few minutes alone,' said Okwaho.

Gad noticed A.G. scowling at his phone.

Lance rubbed his thumb over A.G.'s knuckles. 'Baby, what's wrong?'

'Morgan's not returning my texts.' A.G. looked at Lance. 'Babe, I'm worried.'

'You want to pass by her place and see if she's okay?' Lance asked softly, his voice soothing. A.G. nodded.

'I'll send Aylmer a message that we've gone,' said Gad.

* * *

Morgan nervously paced to and fro. She had rehearsed what she would say, but she knew it probably wouldn't play out that way. Once Moe came home, she bade him sit in the living room with her.

'What's going on now, Mom?' Moe crossed his arms.

'I need to tell you something . . . *show* you something.' Moe merely looked at her expectantly. 'We are . . . special, you and I. We have that which most do not possess.'

'Wealth?'

'Magic.'

Moe burst out laughing, tilting his head back. 'Have you been reading those Arthurian books again?'

'Moe, we *are* from the Arthurian legends. We are reincarnations, and you and I possess great magic.'

'Okay, you need to tell me what you're on and give me some, stat. Sounds like one hell of a trip.' He shook his head, amused. 'I want in.'

'All right, I will give you this.' Morgan held out her hand to Moe, indigo magic coalescing into a sphere as it emanated from her palm.

'Whoa, that's way cool! What's it do, and how are you doing that?'

Morgan placed her glowing hand on Moe's head, focusing on her knowledge of who they were, who they are now, and—

A force pushed her away so powerful that she landed across the room, slamming into the wall. When she looked back at Moe, his hand was up, palm outward, black pulsating magic swirling like a vortex at his fingertips.

He sneered. When he spoke, his accent was crisp, almost identical to the one from their past lives. 'Thank you, Mother, for allowing me to reclaim my trapped memories. You have done me a great service.'

The smirk on his face made Morgan's blood run cold.

Moe tilted his head to the side. 'Why do you tremble, Mother? *You* are the one who taught me my magic . . . in our other life. Why would you fear me?' He narrowed his eyes. 'Unless you were hoping I'd see Sean for who he was, an evil sorcerer, and side with . . .'

His sneer was mocking. Morgan whimpered in fear. 'Oh, do you really think your magical fluctuation to bring back my memories didn't reveal *your* secrets?' Moe laughed hideously.

Morgan pressed herself against the wall, gasping in shock. 'What have I done?' she whispered.

Moe snarled. No, the being before her was not her Moe – it was Mordred. 'You've ensured the deaths of the Knights of the Round Table, Mother. You've ensured Arthur Pendragon is killed yet again.'

As Mordred pushed his palm towards Morgan, a blast of dark magic struck her, pinning her further. She yelped. Blinking away her shock, Morgan lifted her hands to create a magical barrier that absorbed her son's magic, pushing back against his power.

A snake of lightning danced across the floor and whipped Mordred in the chest. He let out a harsh scream before blue fire whizzed towards Morgan. She ducked, the top of her hair singed by the magical flame.

Mordred swirled his magic about him, wind picking up everything in the room. Determined, Morgan anchored herself solidly to the floor, summoning her own powerful magic.

* * *

'We're not far now,' said A.G., reassured at the thought.

Gad shivered. 'Why didn't we take a car, any car? It's so cold.'

'We once travelled for leagues when there were no cars,' said Lance.

'But now there are! Just because we remember who we were in our past lives doesn't mean we stop living in the twenty-first century . . . mate!'

'Hey!' A.G. scowled. 'Lance is *my* mate and only mine.'

'I meant it in the platonic way. And besides, I'm not into guys,' protested Gad, rolling his eyes.

Okwaho and Serena chuckled as Vivian sighed dramatically.

A.G.'s phone rang; he brought it up to his ear. 'Gen? Is everything okay?'

'No!' she squealed. 'Aylmer's gone AWOL!'

'Wait, what? How do you know? He was with us, like, forty minutes ago.' A.G. stopped and everyone huddled around him.

'He messaged me, saying he didn't want to be Merlin. He said he was going to leave and wipe his entire memory with his magic.' Gen started sobbing. 'I think he's going to do something stupid. I'm so scared.'

'Okay, Gen, don't worry – we're just going to check on Morgan real quick and then we're going to go find Aylmer,' A.G. reassured her.

Lance was already on his phone, shaking his head and shrugging. 'Lance is calling him now. Gen, we're going to find him, I promise! Okay?'

An explosion of shattered glass drew their attention to the colourful lights clashing in the mansion not far from where they stood.

'Shit! That's Morgan's house!' A.G. gaped at the sight. 'Gen, we gotta go, but I'll call you right back after we've dealt with this, okay? I promise!'

* * *

Aylmer stood at the train station holding his ticket, replaying his message to Gen over and over in his head.

Gen, I love you so much, but I am just so scared to die. If I'm not Merlin, then I can't die. If I don't have my memories or magic, then I'm not a threat nor a target. But the only way I know how to wipe my memory is to wipe it all. I won't know who I am, not even in this life. I won't remember you.

I'm so sorry, Gen. I just can't do this. I wanted to spend the rest of my life with you, but this fear hurts me physically. It's debilitating me. And it's been getting worse every day. I can't do it anymore – I can't do this, I can't be Merlin.

I'm sorry. I love you. Perhaps we'll meet again and I'll fall in love with you anew. Until that time, mi amor . . . goodbye.

Aylmer put a hand to his mouth as tears poured down his face. He was shaking so badly.

Taking a deep breath, he began summoning his magic . . . for the last time.

CHAPTER NINE

A.G., Lance, Gad, Vivian, Serena, and Okwaho rushed into the mansion to find Morgan and Moe in the heat of battle. Lightning flashed, hitting Moe in the chest and sending him stumbling, but a vortex around him absorbed most of it. He retaliated quickly with a crackle of dark energy that lifted Morgan off the floor and slammed her back down.

Okwaho sent a burst of green magic towards Morgan, healing her wounds instantly, and then sent a firebolt towards Moe. The others either ran to Morgan's side or attacked Moe the only way they knew how – with their fists.

Vivian lifted her hands and sent droplets of water raining down on them. With a wave of Moe's hand, the water gathered and encased Vivian in a bubble where swirls of black magic laced around the Lady of the Lake, rendering her immobile. She pushed the water magic outwards but fell to her hands and knees, weakened and breathing heavily.

Lance grabbed Moe from behind as Gad kicked his shins, sending Moe to his knees. A.G. thrust his elbow into Moe's neck while Okwaho summoned an orb of crystalline magic and touched it to his back. The young man screamed in agony, but again, the magic trickled into the vortex.

Recovering, Moe punched upwards, taking a stunned Okwaho off guard. The Mohawk teetered back and kicked the other sorcerer in the stomach, sending him staggering back. Moe jumped up, grabbing Lance's arm as the man punched him, and pulled so hard that Lance flipped and fell flat on his back.

Reaching into his jacket, Moe produced a black handgun and spun to push A.G. against the wall, bringing the muzzle to his throat just below his chin. With a click, he removed the safety.

Everyone froze.

'At point-blank, nothing will heal you, Arthur Pendragon.'

A.G. let out a shaking breath, bringing his arms up in surrender. Gad helped Lance to his feet, the First Knight trembling nearly just as much as A.G.

As Okwaho discreetly tried to summon more magic, Moe's gaze snapped to him. His eyes went completely black, their whites, irises, and pupils gone, and pain shot through Okwaho's entire body. The Mohawk screamed, folding in on himself. He took a steadying breath to heal himself.

'Before any of you do anything else, I want you to realise, *Mother*, the power you've unleashed.' Moe pressed the gun harder into A.G.'s throat, causing him to wince.

Moe only smirked. 'A king, squirming in my grasp.' His grip was firm, and his finger remained on the trigger. Disarming him would not be easy.

Lance let out a feeble whimper. Moe's gaze darted to him, eyes still black, and with a grin so frightening that Okwaho shivered. Lance cowered, taking a step back.

'Mordred, stop this at once,' ordered Morgan.

Moe clicked his tongue. 'No, Mother, I shan't.'

'Mordred, listen to me! Sean has fed you lies. You do not have to be the sorcerer you were before – you are a new man now. You are my son, and I will not let the likes of Sean taint your mind!'

Moe tilted his head back, laughing. 'What is this? You think just because Sean recognised my magic, my true identity while I did not, that *he* was using *me*?'

The way Moe emphasised his words gave Okwaho pause.

'You seem to think that Sean is the more powerful of us two. You are sorely mistaken.' His black irisless eyes turned back to A.G. 'I created Sean with *my*— dark magic.'

Okwaho could only gape while the others gasped. In his periphery, he realised Serena was slowly inching her way closer to Moe. Without even glancing her way, Moe lashed out a hand, grabbed her by the throat, and slammed her against the wall. She collapsed to the floor with a yelp, moaning and curling in on herself. Before Okwaho could step in, Moe had his dark-magic eyes on him again and the sorcerer froze in place.

'How?' demanded A.G., his voice a harsh whisper.

Moe grinned, looking pleased. 'I created particles of dark magic – a fluctuating, electrifying orb of dark magic – but I could never complete my ritual. I was attempting to create the most powerful spell to enhance myself, allowing me to become the most powerful sorcerer of all time.' He chuckled deep in his throat. 'It seems that orb did not dissipate when I died. It merely continued gathering its energy.'

His voice resonated with a new, dangerous timbre. 'It created Sean. It . . . *is* Sean. Thus, I— created Sean.'

A.G. swallowed loudly, his Adam's apple pressing against the gun.

'So long as Sean lives, he fuels my power. And if he is destroyed, I absorb it all and become the most powerful sorcerer to exist.'

'I don't think so, asshole!'

A wall of fire instantly razed the entire room, pushing towards Moe with a roar and growing with every inch it advanced until it engulfed the entire room. The flames lifted Moe into the air, and as he ascended, the gun fell and skittered across the flaming floor. No one except for Moe was affected by the spreading fire as he thrashed and wailed, hanging upside down in the fire's grip.

Standing at the front of the room, arms outstretched with his palms up, fire magic streaming from both hands, was Aylmer, his mouth curled into a determined sneer. As he concentrated, the fire burst with another roar – Moe cried out again. The vortex swallowed much of the flames, but there was too much power flowing through the room even for his entropy. As the fire grew, the vortex fizzled with a *pop.*

Aylmer pulled back, bringing his arms in, and the fire dissipated. Moe remained moaning in pain on the floor.

'Aylmer!' cried A.G.

Aylmer's face was contorted in anger, jaw clenched, as he strode towards Moe. He pulled his arms back again, his fire raging. He punched down, his fist and fire hitting and engulfing Moe – but nothing happened.

Moe laughed, sneering. 'You knights never learn. I cannot be killed so long as Sean exists! But kill Sean, and you make me the most powerful sorcerer to exist.'

'I. Don't. Think. So!' seethed Aylmer. '*Asshole!*'

A.G. quickly grabbed the gun off the floor and pressed it to Moe's temple. 'I'll call your bluff.' He looked up. 'Morgan?'

'Do it.' She buried her face in Vivian's shoulder.

Okwaho turned away as the gunshot resounded through the room. The laugh that followed churned his stomach more than any gruesome scene ever could.

He looked back as dark magic surrounded Moe, seeping from those black irisless eyes.

The young sorcerer stood. 'As I said, you never learn. Good luck now . . . for your demise shall be so agonising, you'll *beg* for the release of death.' He glanced at his mother, whose face was streaked with tears. 'You chose the wrong side, Mother. I'll remember that.'

With a cloud of dark magic, Moe was gone, his footsteps receding and his magic trailing behind him as he ran. Morgan collapsed, weeping. Serena pushed herself to her feet and joined Vivian by Morgan's side, while Gad offered the woman his arm for support.

Lance pulled A.G. to him and kissed him so fiercely, his sob sounded like a moan. The two men took a moment to hold each other tightly, their love emanating so strongly, it was stirring to witness. Then they sob-laughed in relief, foreheads leaning together, before they drew back.

A.G. ran to Aylmer, wrapping his arms around him tightly. 'Aylmer, goddamn it, you saved my life. Fuck, what happened to you?' He pulled away. 'Gen said you went AWOL.'

Aylmer sighed, bringing a hand to his forehead. 'There I was, ready to commit magical suicide, and then I realised that the fear I was feeling was so intense, it almost felt unnatural, and a thought occurred to me: I'll just be easier to kill without my magic and if I don't know who I am. That's when it hit me.'

As if to emphasise his point, now back to his normal self, he pushed his glasses up.

'Moe or Sean must've used their magic to cause you to flee,' Okwaho surmised.

'Oh, it was definitely Moe.'

'No, it wasn't Moe.' Morgan stood and pulled away from the others. She took several steps towards Aylmer. 'It was Mordred.'

Okwaho nodded his understanding.

'The minute I helped him remember, he stopped being Moe and became Mordred again. I felt an uncontrollable fear . . . I was trembling from head to toe.'

'That's a bit how I felt it, too,' confirmed Aylmer.

'My healing subdued it, but I felt it as well.' Okwaho remembered the wave of dread that had momentarily frozen him in place.

Aylmer sighed. 'I'm sorry I caused you all such heartache at the thought of me abandoning you.'

'Dude!' exclaimed Gad. 'We were all toast until you showed up.'

Aylmer smirked playfully. 'Sure that's not the other way around? I'm pretty sure I had fire lapping at all the walls in here when I made my epic grand entrance.' He grinned, placing his fists on his hips.

Gad walked over and playfully punched him in the arm. The two embraced. 'You know who you really need to apologise to.'

Aylmer nodded, sobering. 'I know.'

'So, like . . .' started Vivian, rubbing her forehead, 'I remember now why I split my soul.'

<u>Chapter Ten</u>

Everyone else was already at Casey's when the group arrived with Morgan in tow. Aylmer even clocked Isabelle sitting beside Tristan. The only one missing was Devon. Aylmer's heart raced hard as he scanned the room for Gen.

'Say that again,' Gad said. 'That was *cleansing* fire? Shit, I don't want to know what your lethal fire's like.'

'I wanted to avoid friendly fire damage.' Aylmer laughed at his own explanation. 'It would only affect the corrupt and evil souls.'

'Then that should confirm to all of you my true intentions,' stated Morgan.

Aylmer's eyes finally landed on Gen, who stood and dawdled towards him. The rest of the world dissolved around them as he took in her tear-stricken face.

'Gen,' he sighed, '*mi amor*, I am so, so sorry. Saying evil magic was influencing my mind is a poor excuse . . . I am too powerful to let that affect me.'

'Someone's getting cocky,' he heard Gallagher mutter.

'Shut up, let them have their moment,' Boris muttered back.

Aylmer got down on one knee. 'Please forgive me. You are my world, my life. I love you so much.'

'I love you, Aylmer.'

Those simple words filled him with relief. 'Let me bind myself to you with my magic.'

Gen's eyebrows lifted. 'What will that do?'

'It will ensure you always know where I am through magic, until the day I can promise you a future – once we have secured that future.'

'Only if that's what you want. You are a free man.'

'I am a free sorcerer. This will not change that, but it will connect us. I will also know where you are if ever we are separated. Are you okay with that?'

'My answer is the same as it was at the hotel, and the same as it will be for our future.' She gazed down at him. 'Yes.'

Aylmer rose, already summoning his magic in his hand. The glow of cyan magic shimmered like crystal shards, twinkling in and out of existence. He opened his palm, presenting it to Gen, and she placed her hand atop it. They clasped their hands, and as the magic connected them, he sealed her mouth with a tender kiss that deepened by the second.

Wrapping their arms around each other, they continued their breathless exchange with a soft hum that caused Aylmer's stomach to flutter.

'Ahem,' said Lamar, placing his steepled hands between them and gently pushing them apart. 'As sexy as it is to watch the two of you . . .'

Aylmer remembered where they were and scratched the back of his head.

'For a moment there, I thought you were going to propose,' said Tristan.

Aylmer smiled as Gen beamed at him. 'We're going to make sure I can once we've defeated our enemy.'

'And Aylmer already knows what my answer will be.' Gen wrapped her arms around him, hugging him tightly.

Holding hands, they moved to sit together on the large couch beside Raven, who nudged Aylmer and winked, giving him that knowing smirk. Aylmer chuckled at his friend's tease.

'So she's not going to betray us this time?' asked Percy.

'*She*,' Morgan began pointedly, 'just nearly died at the hands of Mordred.'

'I used cleansing fire.' Aylmer glanced Percy's way. 'It would have harmed her otherwise. Her allegiance to us is legit.'

'What happened?' asked Boris. 'Casey just told us to get our asses here ASAP.'

'Mordred has been awakened,' said A.G.

'Oh, we're not even calling him Moe anymore, then?' said Gareth.

'No, we are not,' Morgan replied. 'My son, the moment I showed him the truth, stopped being Moe. He was intent on killing all of us. I . . . thank you for coming and risking your lives for me.'

'Are you kidding?!' exclaimed Serena. 'No offence, but you wouldn't have been able to hold your own against . . .

that. His eyes . . .' She turned to the group. 'His eyes, it was – that wasn't . . .'

Casey waved his phone, getting the group's attention. 'Devon just got out of the OR. He's on his way.'

As they waited for Devon to arrive from the hospital, the group made small talk.

'I'm telling you, it'll be nice to see Sean get what he deserves,' stated Bedford. 'Oh, and' – he grinned – 'I've ordered myself an authentic hook for the fight. I'll be the Pirate of the Round Table!'

'I saw an image of the one he ordered,' said Lamar. 'It's snazzy.'

'It's shiny, sharp, and has a fancy cuff,' said Bedford.

The door opened, and in walked Devon. 'Okay, what did I miss?'

'Moe is now Mordred,' said A.G. 'Oh, and we can't kill him until Sean is dead, but killing Sean makes him absorb all the magic and become all-powerful.'

'And you're just going to believe him?' the doctor asked with scepticism as he joined the group on the plush beanbag chairs.

Aylmer sighed. 'We tried to kill him. A fireful fist didn't do it.'

'Neither did a bullet to the head,' said Lance.

'When the hell did you get your hands on a gun, Pop? You're not a legal gun owner!'

'It was Moe's, and A.G. pulled the trigger.'

'When did Moe get his hands on a gun, and where is that gun now?' demanded Gallagher.

A.G. produced the weapon from his coat pocket. As Gallagher rose and extended his hand expectantly,

A.G. handed it over. Gallagher checked the magazine and unloaded the pistol with expert efficacity.

'You can't hold this if you don't know how to use it. Honestly, you'd have hurt yourselves more than him!'

'You know how to wield a gun?' asked A.G.

'Not by choice. I never thought I'd touch one of these ever again, but if I'm the only one who's had training, then, yeah.'

Serena deliberately cleared her throat, wagging her finger. 'Certified *and* a trainer.' She pointed at herself. 'Or did you forget my squad of armed troops?'

'When did you get training?' Lance asked Gallagher.

'Going from foster home to foster home,' replied the young man. 'A teen shouldn't have to know how to wield a gun to feel safe – not in our country, anyway – but that's how it was. It is what it is.' He sat back down.

'You omitted the most important detail, A.G.,' said Okwaho. 'Sean was created by Mordred's magic.' Everyone gasped. 'An orb of dark magic that has lingered and travelled over the centuries. Sean's existence fuels Moe – Mordred – and killing him will render Mordred all the more powerful. Sean believes himself all-powerful already, but he is the puppet, not the other way around. And, like A.G. said, to kill Mordred, we must first kill Sean.'

The Mohawk man sighed, 'My former mentor will not be easily destroyed. It will require all of us – weapons or no, magic or no.'

'I don't know what I can contribute,' began Isabelle, 'but I will help in whatever capacity I can.'

'Already more knights have been . . . remembering who they were,' said Gad. 'That'll be helpful.'

'We've already begun crafting weapons at the shop,' added Garrick. 'For whatever damage they can contribute to ensure the deaths of our enemies, they will. They are authentic and expertly made. Now I remember why I've been so good with wood and metal in this life!'

'Not only do you know how to wield weapons, but you also know how to craft them,' confirmed Tristan.

'I can inform my division,' said Serena. 'We are a secret unit, but I'm certain the RCMP will cooperate . . . or at least I'm hoping they will.'

'They're likely to arrest Sean and Moe instead,' complained Gareth. 'That won't solve the issue. We need to destroy them once and for all, and well, technically, the battle that awaits us is hella illegal.'

'Fuck the legalities! We've got to save the world,' began Aylmer, 'because magic or not – Sean created by Mordred's magic or not – Sean *is* that orb, those particles of dark magic, black antimatter, black holes. And once Mordred absorbs him, that vortex he was creating? It'll be powerful enough to suck the world in *whole* if we don't kill him immediately after.'

'I will ensure with all the legal power I possess that you will not be pursued for this,' Serena asserted.

'People are gonna know magic exists,' said Percy. 'They're gonna know that we're reincarnations of the Knights of the Round Table.'

'Is that such a bad thing?' asked Casey.

'It will make some of us more popular,' admitted Devon.

'And some of us more harassed,' said Raven, though he was grinning.

'Shut up, you love the limelight,' teased Garrick.

Aylmer realised that up until now, they had all been strategising, but Vivian had not said a word – she looked like she was patiently waiting.

After a few more exchanges, the group grew quiet. As Vivian stood, all eyes turned to her and she began to glow, ethereal and transparent. A figure stepped out of her corporeal form and stood in the middle of the place – a younger version of herself, draped in a blue robe of shimmering magic, long hair cascading to her feet.

The room was filled with the vision as Vivian narrated her past.

'When Mordred died, his orb dissipated, but not entirely.'

Floating in the centre of the room was a translucent black orb, crackling with magical lightning. As Vivian continued, the orb grew bigger and crackled louder and louder.

'As Mordred told us, over the centuries, it travelled through the world, gathering magic and power, and eventually, it created Sean. This brought Mordred back to this world, and the rest of you. As for me . . .'

The vision shifted back to the ethereal, youthful woman Aylmer knew to be the Lady of the Lake's true form. She had her head bowed, her eyes closed, and as Vivian resumed, the woman began to glow more brightly.

'I knew of this orb of dark magic and that it persisted, despite Mordred's defeat. I performed a ritual to split my soul and be reborn in reincarnations of myself so that I might protect the world from Mordred's evil magic.'

The vision of the Lady of the Lake split into the many iterations of herself, all standing around her original form, all of them of various ethnicities, various ages, wearing different garb – all of them women.

'Every time, I was born where the orb of dark magic resided, or moved to live where it existed if it travelled after my birth. I moved from the Carolinas to Canada without realising I was following the orb, but I remember being nomadic in all my reincarnations, never settling for too long in one place. Whether I knew it or not.'

The figures in the vision all merged with Vivian once again before fading completely from view.

Her eyes scanned the group. 'I don't know what I would have done to protect the world, but it seems my magic ensured it couldn't grow too fast.'

'It's possible it kept moving to get away from you,' suggested Okwaho.

'I don't see why anything or anyone would want to escape this gorgeous woman,' said Gad, staring wistfully at Vivian. All eyes turned to him. The man cleared his throat. 'I said that out loud, didn't I?'

Vivian took his hand. 'That's sweet.'

'When Sean was born, you must've felt compelled to move up here,' voiced Isabelle.

'Must be. Why else would I choose to endure such freezin' cold Canadian winters?' Vivian shrugged.

'If you return to your true body, or incorporeal form . . .' began Raven.

'It must be done after Mordred's and the orb's destruction *and* while I remember myself, though I can do it anytime and anywhere.'

Aylmer stood. 'I'm not going to let that dark being who calls itself Mordred kill us – magically, physically, or mentally.'

He glanced at his friends, determination burning within every ounce of his being. A.G. stood to join him.

'Destroying Mordred the first time a millennium and a half ago failed because he created his orb of magical particles,' Aylmer explained, growing excited. 'This time, if we want to destroy him for good, we must destroy that orb – Sean. Then, if Mordred absorbs it into himself, killing him should end him *and* his magic for good.'

'And I won't let him kill you, A.G.,' declared Lance, taking his boyfriend's hand in his. 'Not again.'

'Nor will I.' Gad moved to stand by their side.

'You have my allegiance,' asserted Morgan, also standing.

'And mine,' said Okwaho. Serena echoed the sentiment.

As everyone stood, Aylmer felt himself tremble with magic the same way he had the first day it returned to him. But this time, he knew it was his power, and he did not fear it – he embraced it.

'We are the Knights of the Round Table!' A.G. called out.

'Yeah!' everyone shouted.

'We are valiant, we are strong, and we believe in fighting for the truth and for loyalty. In this life, we fight not for one kingdom – for Camelot – but for the entire world, for our planet, and perhaps the entire universe. Whatever life lies beyond our atmosphere, it shall be saved. And I, Arthur Gabriel . . .' – he smirked – 'Arthur Pendragon, will lead the charge against our enemy!'

'And we shall follow you!'

'And why will we succeed? Why will victory be ours?' demanded A.G.

He lifted his fist high, even if he did not wield his sword, as he and everyone present shouted, 'Because we are the Knights of the Round Table!'

A.G. walked down the middle of the street, approaching where Mordred and Sean awaited him. The reincarnated King was flanked by Lance and Aylmer while the other knights marched behind him – his Knights of the Round Table.

The asphalt beneath his boots crunched from the packed snow and black ice that glazed it. Cold wind whipped his face, but the air of winter was subdued by the adrenaline already coursing through his veins.

Serena and her connections had ensured the streets were closed off. The Royal Canadian Mounted Police had been advised and made privy to what would be happening today – a battle between sorcerers and reincarnated knights, a battle to the death, a battle to stop evil from creating a literal black hole that would destroy the world if not the entire galaxy. It had been a lot for some to take in, imminent potential apocalypse aside, but the knights had their cooperation.

Each knight was armed – A.G. held Excalibur, Lance wore a shield Gad had made him strapped to his back, and Gad and his brothers each wielded spears. The others were equipped with a variety of weapons, some modern, some medieval, all matching their unique skills from both their lives.

Holding Excalibur aloft, A.G. stopped several metres away from the wicked pair. Sean had a snarl on his face, while Mordred's eyes remained blackened.

His heart was racing and drumming hard on the inside, but on the outside, A.G. was calm, his grip on his sword steady. Lance reached for his hand and squeezed gently, letting him know he had his First Knight and lover with him. To A.G.'s left, Aylmer flicked his hand, and a large flame appeared. The flame burned red, and it seemed to A.G. as though the flame dissipated any and all doubt.

Without taking his eyes off his enemies, A.G. whispered a quick thank you to his friend.

Mordred straightened as he and Sean observed the group.

'So many knights following their King to their deaths,' Mordred called out. He clicked his tongue. 'Their blood will be on *your* hands, Arthur Pendragon.'

'Victory will be ours today, because we have that which unifies us,' declared A.G.

Sean snickered. 'Let me guess, love?'

'Loyalty, and honour.'

'We'll just see about that. We'll see how much *honour* they have when they look death in the eyes. Some of them already have.' Sean glanced at Bedford. 'And have whimpered in their terror.'

Bedford sliced the air with his hook. 'Try that again, Sean, and see where my hook lands. You might have dismembered me once, but I am a survivor, and I wield the weapon that will cleave you to your death.'

Sean let out a sinister laugh. 'Sure, we'll go with that.'

They all took a moment to assess each other.

'I'm disappointed, Mother, that you would choose them over me. You let them try to kill me the other night.'

'Mordred, you are inhuman – you are evil incarnate. Your existence and magic threaten more than a group of knights. Much more is at stake here. I cannot allow you to continue. I might have given birth to you, but I will see to it that your magic ends today.'

Mordred scoffed, folding his arms. 'I thought it would always be you and me, Mom.' His eyes regained their human form, and for a moment he looked like Moe again.

'I thought so too, my son. I . . . I love you – you are my son.'

'You love me, yet you would see me killed!' spat Mordred, his eyes returning to their dark magic state.

'It is because of the love I have for you that I will stop you before you become worse than what you are now, before you destroy this world. You must be stopped. Both you and your creation.'

Mordred tilted his head to Sean as the two sneered.

'How does it feel, Sean, to know that you were created by an orb of magic? How does it feel to know that you are not the most powerful sorcerer among us?' Aylmer called out.

'I feel that it's time you learnt your place, Merlin. You are nothing more than mere energy for me to absorb. As for you, Okwaho' – Sean turned his gaze to the Mohawk sorcerer – 'I am disappointed in you. Who was it who taught you to control your magic and utilise it in powerful ways?'

Okwaho remained stoic. 'That no longer matters. I saw early on what you are, even if I did not fully understand it at the time.'

Mordred made a big show of yawning, leaning his elbow on Sean's shoulder. 'Are we done here? Can we get to the part where I kill you all?'

As if moving with inhuman speed, Mordred transposed several feet forward, sending tendrils of black magic out towards the knights. At the same time, Sean dispensed a cloud of sizzling energy.

Immediately, Vivian lifted her arms and water rained down around the cloud of magic, drenching it. The cloud darkened and began to hover above the ground, slowing as though weighed down.

Aylmer cast a wall of cleansing fire that roared across the asphalt. It burnt any and all impurities in its path, shrinking the ice beneath it to a thinner sheen and evaporating some of the snow. Once it reached their enemies, the fire burnt even brighter, ready to deliquesce the entropy.

Sean grunted in discomfort as he leapt out of the fire's path, while Mordred lashed out at it with his tentacle magic, releasing an inhuman hiss.

The fire dimmed and lost its puissance.

A.G. lifted Excalibur, catching one of the tendrils. The black tentacle coiled around the sword and he pulled, yanking and ripping the tentacle in two. Another tendril, A.G. whacked before a colourful bolt of magic sizzled past his head. He locked eyes with Sean.

'If that's how you want to play it . . .' A.G. muttered to himself.

Sean cast another stinging bolt of magic that A.G. easily batted away with his blade, sending it back to the sorcerer only for him to absorb it before creating another.

'Fun! Didn't realise you were into sports.' With a two-handed grip, A.G. batted away another bolt.

'Let's see how long you can last.'

Devon skidded to a halt behind Sean, wielding a knife. His face was twisted in concentration. A.G. knew the doctor had precise knowledge of exactly where to cut to make it hurt, to make it bleed, to sever veins and tendons.

Making a swift calculation, Devon sliced at Sean. The dark sorcerer jumped back, spinning, giving A.G. a brief moment of reprieve from the magical bolts.

Devon ducked as Sean lashed out with his magic and sliced Sean's leg, ripping the denim and lacerating his flesh. Sean cried out as blood spurted from the wound.

Then the sorcerer, pushing Devon off him, began to laugh as his blood floated into the air. The flowing crimson gathered into one massive pool that Sean drew back into himself, like drops of red sweat being soaked up into his pores. The gash visibly healed within seconds and blood stopped flowing. Any that lingered in the air, Sean absorbed.

'Crap – backfire.' Devon sidestepped as Sean lunged towards him.

The sorcerer pounded a fist to the ground, cracking the asphalt and causing the ground to quake.

Sean's glee was a reverberating roar. 'You've just made me stronger!'

Sneering, Sean punched the pavement again and the doctor lost his footing, falling to the ground. Casey slid in, the ice making it look like it was a fluke, and jabbed an elbow at Sean. Sean spun around, magic crackling at his fingertips.

Casey reached up and grabbed the bolt of magic with his hands, holding it like he would a ball. His eyes widened, and he whooped out a laugh.

'I guess I do have some magical abilities!'

'It won't be enough to save your life.'

Hugging the orb of sizzling magic, Casey tackled Sean and rammed the ball into his chest, propelling Sean several feet away. Casey looked pleased with himself.

* * *

The four brothers fought side by side to bat away magical attacks as well as Mordred's physical blows. Armed with the spears they had fabricated themselves, they launched themselves at their enemy, along with several others fighting with them to keep Mordred occupied.

Gad pierced Mordred in the thigh, but it barely made a dent in the young sorcerer's abilities or life force. In fact, Gad couldn't see a trace of blood.

'You're wasting your efforts,' Mordred sneered. 'I cannot be killed!' He plucked the spear out of Gad's hands and snapped it easily in two.

Gareth rushed forward and impaled the eighteen-year-old, launching the spear like a lance. The spear merely slid out through the other side and fell onto the black ice, clanking without a single drop of blood.

'That is just so not normal,' muttered Gareth.

Gad was beginning to grow frustrated, but he preferred to keep Mordred distracted than try to fight Sean; if he got hurt, he wouldn't be able to protect his brothers. He was not going to lose them again, not in this lifetime.

Mordred picked up the spear and slashed at Raven, leaving a small gash on his face.

'Hey!' Raven scowled. 'My perfectly handsome face!' He had that look that told Gad he was trying to keep Mordred's attention occupied – he knew Raven's ego could handle a scratch or two.

Meanwhile, Garrick smashed his spear over Mordred's head. The metal broke, but Mordred grunted in anger, hands flaring up with magic.

'I grow tired of this back-and-forth,' Mordred snarled.

'How about we fight, then, young men that we are? Let the geezers rest a bit.' Gallagher shot Gad a wink, grinning, before turning back to Mordred.

Gad knew what Gallagher was doing – reminding Mordred of his Moe side, his human side, the one who always bickered and snickered and prattled complaints. If it kept him busy and distracted while the others killed off Sean, then all the better.

Mordred turned his attention to Gallagher. The twenty-year-old young man opened his arms up before taking a stance, fists raised.

'Fist to fist, no magic. You best me, we back off.'

Mordred laughed. 'If I best you, you die!'

Mordred punched so hard, Gallagher went flying across the street, winded and gasping. He clutched at his chest, breathing gutturally.

'Gallagher!' Lance ran to his side, helping him up.

'I'm okay, Pop.' Lance put his hands on Gallagher's face, staring into his eyes. 'Lance, I swear, I'm fine . . . Past-Life Dad.'

Lance hugged him briefly before pulling away. Wielding the shield forged by Gad, Lance brought it up to block the spurt of magic that came his and Gallagher's way. Aylmer had imbued it with protective magic, so though it was but a simple wooden shield, it could withstand more than expected at first glance.

Lance sliced the shield through the air at Mordred as the young sorcerer advanced on him. Gad ran forward, his brothers behind him, and pulled Mordred away from the two. Mordred brushed the brothers off him and lifted a fist. Gallagher and Lance lunged out of the way in opposite directions as Mordred sent a wave of black magic towards where they had stood. It latched onto an evergreen tree that instantly withered, cracking, and its needles fell as its greenery blackened.

'Shit,' Gad gaped. 'What do we do now?'

Mordred laughed deep in his throat. 'Now . . . you die.'

'You realise you're violating at least a hundred Canadian laws right now?!'

Mordred paused, scowling, and turned to Serena who stood behind him. In her hand, she held the gun they had retrieved from Moe.

'And you're not?'

Serena flashed him a bitchy smile. 'I have per-mission from the RCMP. And I've got this.' She raised the gun, holding it steady with both hands. 'It was unregistered. Except . . . I have proper training.'

She pulled the safety back. Its click was hollow as the wind howled.

Mordred contorted his face, scrunching his nose in defiance. 'You cannot kill me.'

'I don't need to kill you. I just need to make it hurt.'

Serena pulled the trigger and the bullet passed through Mordred's chest. He grunted, looking infuriated – his expression told Gad indeed, it hurt. Even if they weren't killing him, they were inflicting pain, and if Mordred was busy subduing his pain, then he wasn't coming after any of them.

Serena fired again, this time grazing Mordred's face. 'I've got plenty of ammunition, Mordred. Let's dance.'

* * *

Okwaho countered a spell Sean had unleashed, running in to block it before it could hit Gen. She ducked, voicing her thanks as she and Isabelle spun to get a better angle, both ladies wielding bows.

Isabelle winked at Gen. 'Archery class is paying off *big-time* right now.' The woman aimed high at an electrical wire. The arrow sliced it in two and it came down on Sean, sending sparks flying.

He grunted in discomfort as he moved out of the way, giving Okwaho an opening to cast a disruptor spell. *That should slow him down,* the Mohawk thought.

'Which class?' asked Gen. 'In *this* lifetime or in our previous life?' She bent low, angling her bow sideways, and the arrow whirred through the air, hitting Sean in the wrist and interrupting the spell he was conjuring.

Okwaho couldn't help but admire not only the timing, but the precision these women had. Their technique seemed flawless.

Sean turned his angry gaze to Gen. 'You bitch.'

Within seconds Percy was on top of him, piggyback style, pounding a fist into his back to distract him – which gave Okwaho another opening.

'What did you call her? Huh?! Say it again and see what happens, jerk!' Percy slammed his elbow down onto Sean's neck.

Okwaho summoned his magic, waiting for the right moment. Sean jerked Percy off him, flinging his arms – and there it was, chest open for attack.

Okwaho sent the orange-coloured spell right at Sean's abdomen. Sean screamed in agony, falling to his knees and glaring up at Okwaho. The Mohawk man only shot a look of disdain back at him, conjuring another spell.

Sean placed a boot on the ground, elbow on his knee as he let out a guttural sigh. The wind sang in a low vibration as Sean's incoming spell made everything tremble around them. He rose to his full height as he conjured the spell, puffing out his chest.

Okwaho hoped he had time enough to cast his counterspell. His eyes remained fixed on Sean as he focused all his strength and magic into the disruptor spell. Sean took a menacing step forward, the elder sorcerer's spell nearly ready.

Tristan came bounding towards Sean to stop him, Lamar and Boris at his flanks. The three knights formed a wall, linking arms, and tackled Sean wrestler-style, but the sorcerer swatted them aside with ease. The three knights fell to the ground, groaning.

'Out of my way, you pests!' Sean strode to Okwaho, just as this one unleashed his spell, its fiery orange alighting everything around them.

Sean lifted his hand, catching the spell. The magical energy began to turn a burnt colour, dark and ashen, before Sean unleashed it with a shockwave that shook the ground.

Okwaho staggered back, shocked and dismayed. Before the Mohawk could recover, Sean grabbed him by the neck, lifting him off the ground. Okwaho gasped for air.

'You think you can defeat me? A puny apprentice – *my* apprentice? You forget I am a master sorcerer!'

Okwaho wheezed, attempting to respond.

'You forget I know your secret, Okwaho. It was me who paid for your surgery, after all.'

'That . . . is not . . . your secret to tell.'

'No, but it's mine to exploit.' The glint in Sean's eyes turned sinister, reflecting his malice as he squeezed harder, and Okwaho felt himself weaken. 'Everything you take to be the . . . healthy man that you are, I can extract from your body to make myself stronger.'

Okwaho felt like pin needles were pricking his entire body as his strength began to leave him. It was as though Sean was growing taller – his muscles were enlarging, and he laughed hideously as he flung Okwaho aside. The younger sorcerer gasped in a lungful of air as he landed on his stomach, rolling a few times from the sheer force. His throat and lungs were burning, but he was breathing, and alive.

Sean pounded a fist to the ground, and the shock-wave that rippled out broke the asphalt beneath everyone's feet. It sounded like rocks falling until Okwaho realised they were rising.

Sean lifted his arms in the air and the wind picked up around him. The loose cable lashed out at the knights, jolting them until they fell to their knees as they writhed in pain. Electrical circuits came undone, poles were ripped out of the ground, hitting anyone in their wake, and the broken asphalt rose from the ground to form a barrier around Sean.

That's when Okwaho realised, 'He's desperate. This is our chance – we must end him now!'

Aylmer extended his arms, sending out firebolts at Sean while Morgan snapped her fingers, coordinating her magic with Aylmer's. Every time the two attacked, a piece of asphalt broke down into particles of dirt that rained back down like pebbles. Sean sneered through the gaps with an angry growl.

Bedford jumped atop Sean's shoulders from behind like Percy had, bringing his hook around to the man's throat.

'You've made me the Pirate of the Round Table, and now, it's time to end your malice.'

'Slice my throat and my blood will fuel me! You will not succeed in killing me.'

'That's where you're wrong!' shouted Okwaho.

Everyone paused and turned to him. He took a wide stance. 'I am a healer, Sean, but *you* trained me – therefore, I am also an entropic sorcerer. I can ensure the opposite of healing occurs.' He smirked, lowering his voice. 'And I will ensure it hurts.'

As Okwaho reached out and within, Bedford took the cue and sliced with the tip of his hook. Sean gargled, though the wound healed almost instantly. The blood that had spilled, Okwaho used to poison, to weaken, and to inflict draining magic upon the sorcerer. Bedford jabbed his hook again and again – in the shoulder, in the ribs, and every time, Okwaho entropically turned Sean's blood into a malady to weaken him.

Aylmer continued his fiery onslaught all the while, each bolt singeing Sean more and more.

'Just a few more nudges and he won't be able to heal at all!' Okwaho called out.

'I've got this.' Morgan reached out with one hand as Mordred shouted in frustration, darting towards them and abandoning the group that was keeping him distracted. Morgan put out another hand, shoving her son away with wind magic while keeping her other trained on Sean. 'Allow me to give your hook a bit of a magical boost.'

Bedford stabbed down with the hook's tip, and as Morgan flourished her wrist, the hook went in deeper and Sean writhed in agony, shouting out. He grabbed Bedford by the hook and plucked the weapon out, flinging the knight aside.

Sean's face twisted venomously as he closed his fists. Bedford screamed.

'Fuck! Not this again.'

More knights began to scream, falling to the ground.

Vivian wailed as she fell to her stomach. 'I forgot . . . how painful . . . splitting my soul . . .' She cried out again.

'You all died in agony – you will relive that pain now!' roared Sean.

All at once, Gallagher clutched his heart, Percy grabbed his leg, Lamar's hand shot to his throat, and Devon fell to his side with a wail of his suffering. Isabelle reached a hand out towards Tristan as she cried out – Tristan was moaning as the magic lashed at him. Gen was cradling herself, and Okwaho could tell it pained Aylmer not to run to her.

A.G. fell onto his back, writhing in pain, crying out.

'A.G.!' screamed Lance. He tried to run to him, but he too was afflicted and staggered to his knees, gritting his teeth as pain overtook him.

The four brothers were shouting their agony while Boris, Casey, and Serena huddled together, attempting to growl it out and move past it, but they, too, fell eventually, the pain incapacitating the three of them.

While Serena and Okwaho were not reincarnations, Sean's entropy still enveloped them in torturous sensations, though the Mohawk sorcerer was able to subdue most of it, thanks to his healing.

Aylmer winced but continued his onslaught of fire. He placed a hand on his arm to steady it as sweat beaded on his forehead. He was struggling to maintain his magic, and the fire began to weaken, spurting out sporadically.

Okwaho focused harder. 'One last push. We just need—'

Sean roared, the sound echoing throughout the street, reverberating within the other sorcerer's chest. Face contorted, Morgan let out a high-pitched wail as she fought to maintain her position.

'I can't hold this much longer!'

Mordred was advancing slowly, pushing against the wall of Morgan's magic. She was using bifurcated magic – Okwaho had never been able to master that.

Vivian rose to her hands and knees, crawling slowly towards Mordred. Everyone else continued to writhe in agony on the ground.

The Mohawk sorcerer made eye contact with Morgan. They each nodded, then he made eye contact with Aylmer. Okwaho told himself, *We give it everything we've got, whatever the outcome.*

With a final beat, Okwaho extended both hands, pushing out while pulling on Sean's life force as hard as he could. Aylmer lifted his arms as fire engulfed the entire street.

Vivian stood and shot an onslaught of water at Mordred, freezing it once it met its mark. 'I've got the bastard covered!'

Morgan let go of the wind magic that kept her son at bay and moved both arms towards Sean, dark magic flowing from her hands.

'Now!' Okwaho shouted.

The three sorcerers gave a final push of their strongest magic, hitting Sean with a constant stream of attacks. The entropic sorcerer screamed, deflecting, absorbing, sending it all back, yet they did not relent, no matter how painful. Though Aylmer fell to his knees, Morgan let out another high-pitched scream, and Okwaho winced and grunted, they never ceased pushing forward with their magic.

Black tendrils of dark matter began to seep out of Sean, and his body began to burn and decay. Still, he pressed forward, roaring entropically until he was a pure black swirl of magic, a crackling orb of energy. His skin disintegrated horrifically and his bones snapped before they became ash, joining the mass of dark magic.

Electrifying magic thundered from the cloud of entropy as it floated across the space towards Mordred, lashing out with its black tendrils, whipping at the ground, whipping at the others.

The barrier of ice around Mordred shattered and the young man laughed as he was freed, spreading out his arms to embrace the magic floating towards him. He became still, unmoving as the absorption began.

The knights stopped screaming, pushing them-selves to their feet. At last, Okwaho felt the release of Sean's magic. Aylmer relaxed as Morgan shoved away the tentacles that whipped at her.

The cloud wrapped itself around Mordred, whose black eyes now emitted smoky tendrils of their own. Okwaho lifted his arm to redirect a whipping tentacle.

'My son is absorbing—!' Morgan screamed, ducking.

Aylmer quickly put his hand up, creating a barrier to block the next magical tentacle. Together, he and Okwaho kept Mordred's magic at bay.

* * *

Everyone began moving away from the reach of the dark magic. A.G. was sore but alive, and as he pushed himself up and gathered his bearings, relief washed through his body from the cessation of the pain.

It was like standing in the middle of a storm. The magic was hissing and whirling around them.

'We have to move in closer to create a tighter barrier!' Aylmer shouted.

'Following your lead!' Okwaho confirmed over the din.

Moving as one, Aylmer and Okwaho took careful steps towards Mordred, closing and constricting their magical bubble of fiery and electrifying magic. Before they could close the gap completely, a tentacle lashed out from the cracks, impaling and flying through Lance, who screamed.

Aylmer and Okwaho closed the gap, chancing a glance back, eyes wide in shock.

It felt like time itself had stopped. The black tendril protruded through Lance's back. Morgan yanked it out of existence and Lance fell to his knees first, then onto his back, blood pooling beneath him.

The world stopped and ended before A.G.'s eyes.

'LANCE!' he screamed. The King ran forward, sliding to a halt and dropping to his knees beside his lover. Lance was trembling, struggling to reach out his hand to cup A.G.'s face. 'Lance, baby, stay with me.' A.G. cradled his boyfriend's head.

'A.G. . . . I love you,' Lance said shakily. 'Always remember that.'

'No, no, no!' A.G. wailed in sorrow. Gad sniffed as tears trailed down his face. The others surrounded them protectively. Morgan stopped beside A.G.

Aylmer and Okwaho readied their magic, one hand each still focused on their barrier.

'Your healing magic won't do any good, Okwaho,' declared Morgan. 'Keep your focus on your barrier.' She returned her attention to Lance, crouching beside A.G. 'He's been hit with dark magic, that of the purest evil. Only the sacrifice of another life in exchange for his can save him now.'

A.G. let out a sob, and his tears poured down onto Lance's face.

Lance winced. 'A.G., you've made me so happy.' His voice was a mere whisper now. 'Our life as lovers may have been short-lived . . . but I've loved you a long time. Perhaps even in our previous lives.'

'Lance, I can't lose you. I need you!'

'You heard her . . . nothing will save my life.'

A.G. put a hand to his mouth, sobbing. It felt like the tendril had reached his heart and shattered it into tiny bits of shrapnel.

Morgan glanced behind her at Mordred. The barrier Aylmer and Okwaho were maintaining was holding strong for now, but as Mordred's magic continued crashing against it, it was apparent the barrier would soon break.

Morgan turned back to A.G. She reached into her pocket and pulled out a business card, handing it to him.

A.G. scowled in confusion. 'What's this?'

'My lawyer,' said Morgan. She closed her hand around his as he took the card. 'I went to see him to write my will. I'm entrusting you with more than this knowledge.'

A.G.'s heart sank, despite it all, as he realised her meaning. He heaved a shaking breath. 'Morgan, no – you can't.'

'Yes I can, and I will.' She took A.G.'s hand. 'You need your boyfriend. I need to atone.' She looked down at Lance, who was fighting to remain conscious. 'Only a practitioner of dark magic can save him.'

'What about—?'

'No *what abouts*!' she argued pointedly, staring at A.G. 'My son needs to be destroyed – Lance needs to be saved. A.G., you best make it count when you deliver the killing blow.'

A.G. put a hand to his mouth again, his vision already blurry with all the tears. 'Thank you,' he whispered. 'I'll never forget this.'

Morgan gave him a wry smile before hugging him quickly. Then she retreated, conjuring indigo magic at her fingertips that quickly spread to glow in the centre of her palms. 'It's been an honour, Your Majesty. Brother. Goodbye.'

She pressed her hands to Lance's chest. Both of them screamed from the shock of the magic as it formed an indigo orb between them that crackled dangerously. The glow from the electric orb expanded before it exploded, crackling outwards. Morgan screamed, and Lance gasped.

And then it was over, Morgan slumped onto the ground.

Lance was breathing heavily. A.G. stared between his boyfriend and half-sister.

Lance propped himself up on his elbows, rubbing his chest. 'She did it, she . . . saved my life,' he whispered tearfully, awed.

A.G. pulled him into his embrace, sobbing and kissing him desperately before holding him tight, not ever wanting to let go. They wept and rocked in each other's arms for another moment.

Then A.G. placed a hand on Morgan's body, whispering his thanks once more. She lay motionless, lifeless.

'Let's finish this.' A.G. stood, raising a hand to wipe at his eyes.

He turned to face Mordred, who stood engulfed by his whirlwind of dark magic. A.G.'s voice, despite not being loud, was heard by all through his determination. 'This ends now. This ends here.' He pointed Excalibur straight at Mordred, who was sneering from behind his magic. 'This ends *forever.*'

A.G. began trudging towards Mordred, keeping Excalibur levelled at its target, catching flying magic on it.

'We can't hold this anymore!' cried Aylmer.

'I know what to do.' Okwaho motioned one hand at the gathered knights. 'Your strength lies in your loyalty to your King. It's time to put that strength into practice!'

'A circle around A.G.!' shouted Gad. 'Around the perimeter. We are the Knights of the Round Table – our memories returned when we stood together. We must once again stand together!'

Gad took Lance's hand in his, who took Tristan's, and soon they were all linked. Vivian enforced their circle with water magic that shimmered around them.

Okwaho nodded to Aylmer and let go of the barrier. 'My magic will create a bubble of healing.' Everywhere the magical water touched, warm and somehow dewless, the knights were healed.

'I will cleanse,' declared Aylmer. 'Then Mordred's whirlwind will be penetrable.'

Aylmer took a step back, bringing his hands above his head. An orb of fire expanded from them and engulfed the entire circle, unmarred by the water magic.

Mordred's black magic lashed out at A.G. but it could not reach him, as though glancing off an invisible barrier. A few tendrils managed to pass through the sustained shield, but when they did, any slashes were instantly healed.

A.G. stopped before Mordred, just outside the dark magic enshrouding the young man. A.G. knew – the only way to end Mordred was to enter the vortex.

Lifting Excalibur to shield his chest, the King stepped forward to place one foot in the swirling vortex, acutely aware of his impending vulnerability.

Chapter Twelve

A.G. heard Lance cry his name, but the moment he passed through and into the vortex, all other sound was cut off. Immediately, pain coursed through A.G.'s body. It felt like tiny pieces of glass were piercing him everywhere at once, yet he did not relent, stepping closer to Mordred. The being before him was a twisted version of what his eighteen-year-old nephew once was.

Mordred snarled, his entire body emitting tendrils of dark magic. He stood unmoving as his magic attacked A.G., as though expecting his enemy to fall before him. A.G. nearly did – his knees wanted to buckle beneath his weight, beneath the weight of his purpose, for he knew when he made his strike, it could backfire and kill him too.

He knew his friends' magic would sustain him only for so long before the black matter assaulting him would claim his life.

Heart hammering with adrenaline, A.G. locked eyes with the being before him, the sorcerer transforming into a miasmic ethereal implosion of energy. If A.G. were to die now, he had to make it count, lest the world be swallowed by . . . this.

Grunting in discomfort, A.G. levelled his sword and thrust Excalibur directly through Mordred's heart. The scream that followed was inhuman, layered with a guttural roar. As the vortex stopped swirling around them, A.G. felt the soothing healing power from his friends and his knights.

He pulled out his sword and Mordred dropped to his knees, eyes becoming human again as the magic left his body before his life did. Then the young man slumped to the ground as he bled out, dead.

A.G. took several staggering steps back. The magic in the air dissipated while it hovered above Mordred's body, and then the heaviness that A.G. had felt since all this began lifted and was no more. Mordred was destroyed.

Lance ran to A.G., who stood holding a crimson-dripping Excalibur to the side, breathing heavily, and wrapped his arms around him, tears pouring from his eyes. A.G. leaned his head on Lance's shoulder, wrapping his free arm around him. Lance turned him around in his arms, and the onslaught of kisses that followed was enough to make A.G. forget the battle that had just ensued.

Lance pulled away, laughing sheepishly. It was A.G.'s turn to pull him in for another series of breathless kisses. He leaned his forehead upon his lover's. 'I love you, Sir Lancelot.'

'I love you, King Arthur Pendragon.'

They laughed.

'Okay, Lance, babe, we need to save our old names for our dirty talk, because it's too damn arousing.'

Lance chuckled. 'Whatever you prefer, baby . . . Ar—'

'Lance,' A.G. warned.

'. . . thur—'

'You want me to take you right here or what?'

Lance bit his lip, grinning. 'Fine, have it your way . . .' He leaned in, his lips grazing A.G.'s ear, his whisper tickling it. 'My King.'

A.G. growled in his throat, half in complaint, half in an aroused tease.

* * *

'All right,' began one of the officers, clad in full Mounted Police uniform, as the division of RCMP officers emerged from the streets beyond. 'You may have done us a service – well, shit, you just did something amazing – but we still need to ask you all some questions down at the station and process you properly. It's, uh, protocol.'

'Totally cooperating, officer,' said Aylmer, taking Gen's hands in his, 'but before I answer your questions, I've got one I promised my girlfriend I'd ask again if we survived.'

Gen's eyes twinkled with tears as Aylmer got down on one knee.

'Gen, Geneviève, my Guinevere . . . will you marry me?'

Gen let out a tearful laugh. 'Yes, Aylmer, my Merlin, I will.'

Aylmer stood and wrapped his arms around her, pressing an elated kiss to her lips, feeling so much joy he thought he'd float into the air – and his magic quite nearly activated and probably would have lifted them both off the ground! Aylmer had to control his impulse to unleash the fire of his passion, quite literally.

'Guinevere and Merlin?' exclaimed the officer. 'I thought Guinevere was King Arthur's wife!'

A.G. chuckled as he and Lance approached, arms each around the other's waist, Excalibur nearly dragging on the asphalt behind him in his loose grip.

'In our past lives, she was, but in this one' – A.G. turned his head to a smiling Lance – 'my heart belongs to my Sir Lancelot.'

'Now you're exacting revenge,' Lance muttered, leaning in to kiss A.G.

The officer only blinked at them. His companion was laughing into her hand, failing to suppress her amusement.

* * *

Gad ran forward, wrapping both A.G. and Lance into a tearful hug. 'Gosh, the two of you'll give me a heart attack one day!' He backed away sheepishly. 'Sorry, I just . . . I need my best friend and my King, you know?'

'I need you, too, Gad,' Lance confirmed.

The officer was still muttering to himself.

'Before you go all fanboy on us at the station,' began Raven. He looked past him and towards the other officer. 'Perhaps *you* would indulge me and let me take you out for dinner?'

'And which knight might *you* be?' she asked.

'In this life, they call me Raven, formerly known as Sir Aggravaine.' He grinned. 'You might have seen my face before. I was awarded the Sexiest Black-Canadian Businessman of the Year a few years back.'

'Yeah, yeah, boast to the pretty lady in uniform,' teased Garrick.

The officer smirked, blushing. 'If you cooperate, I might consider it.'

'Oh, score, brother!' Gareth whooped.

Gad laughed at his brothers. 'They never change, nor do I want them to. We might be reincarnations, but we're still who we are in this life, too.'

'Tell me about it! I can't get rid of this darn accent no matter what I do,' said Vivian as she walked towards him.

'Why would you want to get rid of that adorable Southern accent?' Gad placed his hands on Vivian's face, once again forgetting his onlooking friends. 'It's beautiful, just like you are.'

Vivian blushed, and Gad thought she was so beautiful when she did.

'Gad . . . you're a busy man in his forties, and I'm an ancient entity embodied in a woman who's past fifty-five.'

'So? You're gorgeous! Vivian, I'm attracted to you.'

'I got . . .' She lowered her voice. 'Well, you see my fine lines – and I don't just mean my smile lines.'

'And?' Gad furrowed his brows. 'What is this? I don't care how old you are. I am enthralled by you! I just want to be with you and enjoy my time with you before you go back to your true body.'

Vivian's smile softened. 'I intend on delaying that, my sweet knight, I just . . . don't want to hold you back.'

He gently took her hands in his. 'You're not. Let's just enjoy this, whatever this is, for as long as we can. For as long as we have to be together.'

'You askin' me to be exclusive?' Vivian pulled back, folding her arms and looking expectantly at Gad. 'You want long-term?'

Gad shrugged timidly. 'For as long as possible. Yes.'

He became acutely aware of his best friend whispering, 'Go get her, Gad!' followed by A.G. chiding him in a muttered response, 'Let them have their moment.'

Gad blocked them out, his focus on his Lady of the Lake, hoping she agreed to be exclusively his.

Vivian grinned and let out a laugh. 'You wouldn't rather have me as my true self?'

'No. Well, I mean, can you do that – leave the lake? But also, no! I want you just as you are now.' Gad released her hands and brought them up to cup her face. 'My Lady of the Lake, will you be mine for the time you have left, until you must return to your true body?'

'Oh, you know I'm already yours.' She playfully slapped his arm. 'I just wanted to make sure.'

'Mm-hmmm.' Gad leaned forward, knowing she was playing off the needed reassurance as a tease, and kissed her tenderly.

* * *

Bedford affixed his hook. 'Do you not hear the weird clinking sound from inside the hook? I swear, Sean damaged it.'

'The hook's fine,' Lamar reassured as he draped an arm around his roommate's shoulders, feeling grateful he still had his friends.

'You still reeling from what Sean did?' Devon asked them. 'Because I am. And let me tell you, I don't know what I can take for that. Nothing in my training ever prepared me for such an ordeal.'

He exchanged a sideways glance with Lamar, his expression filled with uncertainty. Lamar reached his other arm to pull Devon into an embrace, which the doctor returned, relaxing somewhat.

'Yet we all survived,' said Tristan, holding Isabelle's hand.

Percy and Gallagher skipped over to Aylmer, Gen, A.G., and Lance, shouting out excitedly and wrapping them in tight hugs.

Serena sauntered over, a smug look on her face.

'Somebody looks pleased with herself,' remarked Boris.

'I just ensured the processing in question doesn't take too long. I've given my statement, and since I have special authorisation, I've ensured an insurance plan would cover the costs of any damages done by our defeated foes.' She pointed at Bedford's hook. 'That includes your hook.'

'You heard that?' Bedford smiled bashfully. Lamar suppressed a laugh; the way the two beamed at each other was painfully obvious.

'With your heroics today,' continued Serena, 'I reckon you should have enough for that snazzy futuristic prosthetic you were lamenting would make a dent on your credit card.'

'I ordered it, you know.'

'I know.' Serena clasped her hands behind her back, strolling alongside the group as they began towards the RCMP officers. 'Why do you think I made sure to include it?'

Tristan leaned towards Lamar. 'Is it just me, or . . . ?'

'Totally not just you, mate,' said Boris.

* * *

Okwaho felt a hand on his shoulder and turned to find Casey looking him over, brows furrowed in concern. There was a beat of silence as Casey hesitated.

'So, tell me if this is none of my business, but Sean said some things during the fight. Like, totally tell me to fuck off and mind my own business, but . . . are you all right? Like, are you . . . dying?'

Okwaho was surprised that *that* was what Casey had surmised from the exchange. 'No, I promise I'm fine. I am perfectly healthy.'

Casey looked significantly relieved. 'Oh, thank goodness.'

A small smile crossed Okwaho's face. He was moved. 'I didn't realise you were so worried.'

'Well, you're one of us now, a Knight of the Round Table, so . . .' He smiled warmly in return, taking a step back. 'Well, that's all I needed to know. Unless you want to share more, just . . . I'm appeased.'

Okwaho chuckled. 'I suppose I could tell you, seeing as I've officially moved into your place now. I just haven't told anyone else from my new entourage. I don't feel they need to know right now, you know?'

'Hey, whatever it is, you can trust me. If you'd rather not say, I get it, but just know that I'll respect your needs, whatever that is.'

'I appreciate that. Actually, I, uh . . .' Okwaho glanced around – the two were removed from the larger group and the noise. 'Casey, I'm trans.'

Casey blinked, eyes widening. 'Wow. I am honoured you would trust me with that.' He put a hand to his heart. 'I promise to respect your privacy.'

'I know, thank you. Devon knows, since he treated my arm, but no one else in the group does.'

'I understand.' Casey took a beat. 'So I guess you met Sean during your transition?'

'Yes, at the very start of it. He paid for my top surgery.'

It somehow felt freeing to open up to Casey about it. The man wasn't prying, only asking a few questions, and reiterated he would respect Okwaho's privacy. Okwaho knew he could tell him only as much or as little as he wanted, and he found himself sharing just enough for now.

Casey beamed at Okwaho. 'Thank you for trusting me with this part of yourself.'

'Thank you for understanding and for your genuine interest in learning about this part of me. Honestly, people are usually either too indifferent or they try to know more than I'm ready to share.'

'By all means, tell me if I ever ask too much, or cross a line, or . . .'

Okwaho placed a hand on the knight's arm. 'You are very respectful. Don't worry, I'll tell you if it ever happens.'

* * *

'I was just so scared I'd lose you, Pop!' Gallagher was sobbing like a child as Lance held him in an embrace. 'Like, you're my dad, from our past lives, and I love you, and in this one I'd be homeless or worse, an addict, maybe dead, if it weren't for you. You mean everything to me.'

'I appreciate that, Gallagher. You mean a lot to me, too.'

'I'm so glad Sean and Mordred are dead,' voiced Percy as Lance and Gallagher pulled away. They laughed tearfully, wiping their eyes and looking embarrassed. 'I swear, I wanted to kill Sean,' Percy went on. 'I'm relieved, I'm . . . pumped! That's what I am.'

Gallagher chuckled. 'I'm ready to beat my record at the bar.'

'Easy there,' said A.G., 'we still need to' – he put on a mocking drawl, making air quotes – "follow procedure." Even a king can't get away from Canadian laws.'

He chuckled before sobering as his eyes were drawn to the ambulance a little further down. Someone was lifting Morgan onto a gurney and rolling it into the ambulance. He sighed.

Lance felt a pang of sorrow in his gut, as though something was squeezing right where he had been impaled. 'What she did for me . . .' He looked at A.G.

I'll help with the funeral, whatever you need from me, baby.'

'I appreciate that.' A.G. smiled tenderly. Their tears were still fresh, but the adrenaline was beginning to leave, replaced with relief and gratitude.

* * *

Before the knights left with the officers, engines revved in the distance as two dozen bikers drove their bikes towards the group. Once they got close, the bikers pressed on the brakes and halted, staring at A.G. Everyone tensed.

'Sean's old gang,' muttered A.G.

A tall young woman removed her helmet, swishing her long windswept ginger hair away from her face as she walked towards him. Her companions followed suit, and then she knelt on one knee before A.G., a hand at her back, and bowed, as did all the others.

'We learnt what Sean was and what you planned to do today,' she spoke. 'He revealed to us his plans and Mordred's. We had no idea. If you would have us, we would be honoured to join the Modern Knights of the Round Table.'

A.G. gaped at her. 'Modern, eh? I suppose that *is* what we are.' He cleared his throat. 'Listen, there will be trials, and . . . uh . . . I'm not saying no, but you were in Sean's gang.'

'We understand.' The young woman rose, smirking. 'Whatever it takes to prove to you we are genuine now that we know the truth.'

'Thank you, but . . . why didn't you come forward sooner?'

'We . . .' She looked back at her friends before turning to A.G. again. 'We don't have the necessary training for the kind of battle that occurred here today. And we were uncertain how well received we would have been, not to mention that Sean could have exploited us.'

The reincarnated King nodded. 'I understand.'

The young woman pointed at some of the guys behind her and smiled wanly. 'Some are willing to make amends for their past deeds at the bar.'

The young men cleared their throats. 'We apologise for our disrespect and disruption. We realise our mistake. Our believed superiority was misplaced.'

'Well, I'll be,' whispered Gad.

'Well, Sean was fuelling and triangulating, I suppose. Thank you for admitting your part in his schemes. It will take more to make amends, but . . . yeah.' A.G. nodded cordially. 'We'll talk more soon.'

'Understood. Thank you.'

The young woman turned back to her group and conferred with a man with similar features. The two of them glanced back, both smiling again in apology, and then the bikers were back on their motorbikes, riding away from the scene.

'Did Moe's old gang just swear allegiance to you, A.G.?' Lamar's eyebrows were raised high as he grinned.

'As though a shroud of entropic magic was lifted from their gazes and clarity was regained,' said Okwaho. 'I know many of these bikers. They are not intrinsically bad people, only misguided – as I was for a time.'

'I hope they join us,' voiced Gallagher, staring into the distance at the bikers' receding forms.

'Oh?' Lance nudged his reincarnated son with his shoulder.

Gallagher blushed, his eyes going wide. 'I mean . . . let's go reclaim that trophy!' He turned, beckoning everyone else to follow as the others let out laughs.

* * *

The group sat around a large booth at the bar, free to unwind at last. Vivian was bringing pint after pint of beer and Gallagher chugged each of them down. Everyone cheered him on, banging their fists on the table and shouting, 'Chug, chug, chug, chug . . .'

Vivian slid him another one, and another. 'You've surpassed your previous record . . . hell, you've surpassed our rival bar's record . . .'

Gallagher snapped his fingers, shooting his arms up in victory.

'How are you still standing?!' gaped Boris.

'Because I am a Knight of the Round Table, and that trophy is my Holy Fucking Grail!' roared Gallagher, arms still above his head. Everyone burst into laughter.

'Well, I've changed into my evening hook,' said Bedford, gesturing so it caught the light.

'Your evening hook,' laughed Devon. 'Gonna have one to match each outfit?'

'As a matter of fact, doc, since this one's not lethal, it's just fancy' – the hook had blue squiggles on it – 'I've ordered another lethal one, with a few additional prosthetics. Who knew being the Pirate of the Round Table would have its perks?'

'I'm glad to see you so enthusiastic,' said Lamar, 'but you don't need to change with us, and you don't need any fancy prosthetics. You know that, right?'

'I know, you all accept me as I am.'

'One hundred percent,' asserted Boris.

'Yo, Raven, pass me the salt for my fries!' said Percy as the brothers were joking around.

Vivian returned and slid into the booth beside Gad, who was conversing with Okwaho, Casey, and Serena.

'So Isabella and I have an official date for the wedding,' announced Tristan. He beamed at Isabelle, and the two announced the date together.

Everyone whooped. 'And I scored myself a date with that RCMP officer,' said Raven.

'Do you know her name?' teased Garrick.

'Of course,' Raven scowled. 'I am a gentleman, after all. The sexiest gentleman!'

'Arguably.' Gareth nudged him with his elbow, chuckling.

Aylmer put his phone away, grinning from ear to ear.

'You look pleased with yourself,' noted Gad.

'I am. The Academy of Quantum Physics of Canada has invited me to explain magic!' With a flourish of his hand, a warm blue ember flared in his palm. 'With demonstration, and scientifically.' Still grinning, he bit his lower lip and shimmied his shoulders.

'Mhmm, you're so sexy when you get all *scientificky* like that,' giggled Gen, nuzzling her nose to his.

'I know,' Aylmer purred, nipping at her lower lip and continuing to hold the blue flame in his open palm.

Lance chuckled, and A.G. turned his boyfriend's face away from the other lovebirds to face only him. He looked deep into his lover's eyes. 'Let's do it, too.'

'Do what, kiss?' Lance smiled, leaning forward.

Before he reached his lips, A.G. answered, 'Get married.'

The table grew quiet all of a sudden. A.G. could feel all eyes on him and his madly grinning boyfriend.

'A.G.,' breathed Lance.

'We waited too long to declare our love for each other. And . . .' He blinked back tears to no avail. 'Had it not been for my sister . . . I would have lost you forever.'

Lance took A.G.'s hand in his and interlaced their fingers, staring down at their hands. 'I'll never forget what she did for me. I will not let her sacrifice be in vain. I will cherish every single day of my life . . .' He met A.G.'s gaze, passion burning deep within his eyes. 'As your husband.'

The knights erupted into a ruckus of cheers and roars, and A.G. and Lance hurriedly captured each other's lips – A.G. wasn't certain who had lunged for the other first.

'Everyone's getting married!' shouted Percy.

A.G. prolonged the kiss, not wanting to part from Lance, not even for breath.

'Okay, okay, come on now!' shouted Gallagher.

'No, keep kissing!' shouted Lamar.

Finally, breathless and chuckling, the two new fiancés pulled away, albeit reluctantly. A.G. pulled Lance to him in a hug, leaning into his side as they returned their attention to everyone else.

A.G. lifted his mug of beer. 'To Morgan, who sacrificed herself for the love of my life.'

'To Morgan,' everyone echoed, lifting their mugs and glasses.

'To magic that has returned and enriched us with the memories of our past lives!'

'To magic!'

'To the return of the Arcane that we are!'

'To the Arcane!'

'To love! To honour!' A.G. called out, and everyone echoed again. 'And to us!'

Everyone roared out together, 'The Modern Knights of the Round Table!'

Fun Facts About
the Knights of the Round Table

KING ARTHUR was Uther Pendragon's son and the King of Camelot who married Guinevere. He was brought to a foster family as a child by Merlin. Many legends claim that he had no true heir, for he had no sons.

His reincarnation, A.G. – short for Arthur Gabriel – was adopted as a baby and is the adoptive brother of Casey. He once dated Gen and is now in love with his roommate and childhood best friend, Lance.

* * *

SIR LANCELOT was King Arthur's First Knight and closest friend. In some legends, he was Guinevere's secret lover.

His reincarnation, LANCE, has a second best friend, Gad. He used to have the hots for Gen before he discovered his true feelings for A.G.

* * *

QUEEN GUINEVERE was King Arthur's betrothed and later became his wife. In some legends, she has an affair or a crush on Sir Lancelot.

Her reincarnation, GEN – short for Geneviève – is A.G.'s ex-girlfriend. She is in a relationship with Aylmer.

* * *

MERLIN was a sorcerer who helped King Arthur. He is said to have brought him to Sir Ector as a child and later guided him and fought alongside him against the dark sorcerer Mordred.

His reincarnation, AYLMER, is a science and physics geek, especially when it comes to quantum science. He is in a relationship with Gen.

* * *

SIR KAY was the foster brother to Arthur. He is said to have had mystical abilities.

His reincarnation, CASEY – nicknamed Cay – is the adoptive brother of A.G.

* * *

SIR GALAHAD was said to have been Sir Lancelot's son and to have obtained the Sword of David. He was one of the three knights who left on the quest for the Holy Grail.

His reincarnation, GALLAGHER, was a foster child and found himself homeless at eighteen. Lance befriended him, took him in, and helped him get back on his feet. Much younger than the others, Gallagher teases Lance by calling him Pop. He is one of the resto-bar's top three chuggers and won a trophy during a competition – a golden goblet.

* * *

SIR GERAINT was a Knight of Devonshire. Not much is known about him.

His reincarnation, DEVON, is a general surgeon who works at the local hospital.

* * *

SIR GAWAIN was Sir Lancelot's most trusted friend. In some legends, he is the heir to the throne after Arthur for being Arthur's nephew. He is said to be the eldest brother, with Sirs Gareth, Agravaine, and Gaheris as his younger brothers.

His reincarnation, GAD, is best friends with Lance. He is the eldest brother of Raven, Garrick, and Gareth. The four brothers own a carpentry business and design furniture for clients.

* * *

SIR AGRAVAINE was said to have been the most handsome knight of the Round Table. He was the second eldest brother, with Sirs Gawain, Garehis, and Gareth as his brothers.

His reincarnation, RAVEN, won Sexiest Black-Canadian Businessman of the Year. He has a few tattoos and well-toned muscles. He is brother to Gad, Garrick, and Gareth. The four brothers own a carpentry business and design furniture for clients.

* * *

SIR GAHERIS was brother to Sirs Gawain, Agravain, and Gareth. It is said he was his eldest brother's squire before being knighted. Due to a miscalculation in battle on the part of Sir Lancelot, Gaheris and Gareth died, and Gawain remained bitter towards Lancelot for the rest of his life. Legends claim Mordred took advantage of the rift between Lancelot and Gawain to kill Arthur.

His reincarnation, GARRICK, is brother to Gad, Raven, and Gareth. The four brothers own a carpentry business and design furniture for clients.

* * *

SIR GARETH was the youngest of the four brothers, with Sirs Gawain, Agravain, and Gaheris as his elder brothers. He is said to have been a true gentleman and to have sadly been abused by Lady Lynette. Due to a miscalculation in battle on the part of Sir Lancelot, Gaheris and Gareth died, and Gawain remained bitter towards Lancelot for the rest of his life. Legends claim

Mordred took advantage of the rift between Lancelot and Gawain to kill Arthur.

His reincarnation, GARETH, was in an abusive relationship with his ex-girlfriend. He is the youngest brother, with Gad, Raven, and Garrick as his older brothers. The four brothers own a carpentry business and design furniture for clients.

* * *

SIR BEDIVERE was a fervent supporter from early on and was one of the first Knights of the Round Table. It is said he remained by Arthur's side when he died and during the transportation of his body to the Isle of Avalon. Legends claim he lost a hand in battle.

His reincarnation, BEDFORD, was the victim of a hit-and-run accident where he lost his hand.

* * *

SIR BORS was said to have been the only knight out of the three to have survived the quest for the Holy Grail. Legends claim he was a chaste knight and never married.

His reincarnation, BORIS, is asexual. He is one of the resto-bar's top three chuggers and won a trophy during a competition – a golden goblet.

* * *

SIR LAMORAK was brother to Percival. It is said he excelled at jousting and was one of the fiercest knights of the Round Table. Legends say that he could fight dozens of enemy knights, besting and killing them all.

His reincarnation, LAMAR, tends to single-handedly win in a brawl or fight against any and all opponents. He is the brother of Percy.

* * *

SIR PERCIVAL was said to have been raised alone by his mother and became a chivalrous knight, defending Queen Guinevere from those who offended her. He is one of the three knights who left on the quest for the Holy Grail.

His reincarnation, PERCY, is always defending friends, especially Gen, and putting those who offend in their place. He is one of the resto-bar's top three chuggers and won a trophy during a competition – a golden goblet.

* * *

SIR TRISTAN was sent to bring the future queen, Iseult, to King Mark. Tristan and Iseult fell in love, however, and ran away together. Some stories depict their story as a tragedy where Tristan is executed and Iseult kills herself as a result.

His reincarnation, TRISTAN, had an affair with Isabelle, his boss's fiancée, whom he was sent to pick up at the airport. It was love at first sight for both of them, and they nearly eloped before the affair was discovered. Tristan's boss was also having an affair, and he ended his relationship with Isabelle amicably. Tristan and Isabelle are now engaged, and Tristan is still employed by his boss.

* * *

ISEULT was one of a few names for the betrothed to King Mark. She fell in love with Tristan, who had been sent to retrieve her for the king. They escaped together, though some stories depict their love affair as a tragedy where Tristan is executed and Iseult kills herself as a result.

Her reincarnation, ISABELLE, was engaged to Tristan's boss when she fell in love with Tristan. They nearly eloped together before the affair became known. Her fiancé had also been cheating on her, and they ended things amicably. She is now engaged to Tristan.

* * *

Vivian was one of many names given to the LADY OF THE LAKE. She is said to have been an ethereal entity who helped King Arthur and granted him his legendary sword, Excalibur.

Her reincarnation, who retains the name VIVIAN, moved to Canada from the Carolinas in the United States. She works as a waitress in the resto-bar where the knights often find themselves.

* * *

MORGAN has had various alterations to her name throughout time. She was King Arthur's half-sister, and mother to Mordred.

Her reincarnation, who retains the name MORGAN, is the older half-sister of A.G., who found her when he was searching for his birth parents. She is the president of a lingerie and accessories design company. She is the mother of Moe and raised him herself, managing and building herself up in the world and quickly moving from middle class to rich upper class.

* * *

MORDRED was the son of Morgan. He was a young and powerful sorcerer who defeated and killed King Arthur in battle.

His reincarnation, MOE, is the son of Morgan. He is a troublemaker and lawbreaker as well as the subleader of a biker gang.

* * *

OKWAHO is a sorcerer of Mohawk origin. His name means 'wolf.' He is also a trans man, and he apprenticed under the sorcerer Sean during his early transition.

* * *

SEAN is a middle-aged sorcerer who believes himself to be the most powerful sorcerer alive. He came into existence by the purest, rawest, and darkest of arcane magic. He is the leader of a biker gang.

* * *

SERENA is a Pendragon descendent from a long line that began with King Arthur's daughter. She is the leader of a specialised group of protectors of Arthurian artefacts, and she is a prophet.

<u>THANK YOU SO MUCH FOR READING</u>

If you enjoyed this story,
please consider taking a few moments
to write a review on Amazon or Goodreads.
It would mean so much.

Thank you.

About the Author

Celinka Serre is an indie writer working in freelance and sharing stories of various genres and personal anecdotes on Medium. She believes in the freedom of creativity and always continues to pursue her dreams. Among her many endeavours is *Stardust Destinies*, the first full-length fantasy saga she began writing at age 19. It stands alongside her work in fan-fiction, fiction short stories and novellas, various indie film screenplays, and a few collaborative projects.

Connect with Binky Ink:

WordPress Website & Blog
  https://binkyproductions.com/binkyinkwriting
Medium – Main Profile
  https://medium.com/@BinkyInkWriting
X (Twitter) https://twitter.com/binkyinkwriting